HELL IN HEELS
A
SEX, DRUGS AND ROCK
ROMANCE

J. HANEY
&
S.I. HAYES

This book is a work of fiction. Any similarities to any person, place or theory is in no way intended or to be inferred as fact or reference.
The work is the singular property of the Authors, and may not be reproduced in whole or in part without permission, unless as part of a Review, Interview or Public push of the work and certain other noncommercial uses permitted by copyright law.
Contains adult situations. 17+ only

Cover Design by Author S.I. Hayes
sihayes.com

ii

ALSO BY J HANEY

(Hudson Bros. PI Series)
An Unexpected Love

(A Heart Strings Love Affair)
Kentucky Blues

Written with S.I. Hayes
(A County Fair Romance)
Stolen Moments
Winter Kisses
Spring Fling

(A Sex, Drugs and Rock Romance)
Vegas Lights

ACKNOWLEDGEMENTS

First, we'd like to thank Rebecca Baldridge aka Jess's Mom for being our awesome editor. This story has its moments and leaves you with a Dominant Prick and a Queen Bitch. The question is will Queenie stay on her pedestal? It's time to read and find out!

We want to thank the Beta Readers; Samantha Soccorso, Victoria Berfet, Cheryl Welch-Keene, Carmellia Woods, Carrie Stark Stinmetz, A.D. Herrick, Trish Longnecker-Potter and Yvonne Isakson as well as the Bloggers and Reviewers for being a part of this journey with us!

To our amazing fans: Thank you so much for reading Angelica and Maverick's story. This was something that touched us both and we are grateful to you for coming along for the ride!

J. Haney & S.I. Hayes

Shannon! What can I say about you that I haven't said a million and one times? I suppose something like this... You're one of the bestest friends I could have. Thank you for joining me on this crazy adventure! Dee, GAH! You know I love you and I tell you at least every day. You've become one of the best PA's I could dream of and I can't wait to see what other crazy we can get up to next! Susan, yet another amazing PA! What can I say that I haven't already told you? You make sure I'm pimped everywhere under the sun and I swear watching the notifications pop up make my fingers hurt. I thank God for all three of you because you each make my author life complete.

~ J. Haney ~

Jess, you have a way about you that I adore! A growl in the mornings that I've come to cherish and a goofy giddiness when you're tired that makes working with you worth the sleepless nights! Never change. I love you, kiddo.

Samantha, you rock, girl! More than a PA you've become an awesome friend and PIC. I wish you weren't so far away, cuz you deserve so many hugs!

Cheers!

S.I. Hayes

DEDICATION

This is for all of you who may love a Dominant Prick or Queen Bitch! Either can make your life hell, then at the same time, you wouldn't know what to do without them!

1

ANGELICA

FUCK, WHERE IN THE HELL AM I? I open my eyes and go to rub my head only to feel a pull against my arm. Looking, I see I've got an IV. It's dark in the room, but the smell of antiseptic is a tell. I'm in the hospital. Last thing I remember, I was recording up at the cabin in Aspen. Everyone else had hightailed it looking for Brent, who'd up and split in the middle of the night. My stomach hurts and my legs feel like they're on fire. What are they pumping me full of? I look at the bags, but my vision is blurry. Damn sedatives. There's somebody in the room, but I can't make out who.

"Hello?" I manage with a dry throat. My voice sounds like gravel.

"Easy, Miss Fontaine, you're in Aspen Valley Hospital."

"What? What happened? My voice?"

"You've been heavily sedated while they've been flushing your system. They had to pump your stomach as well. You're being fed intravenously right now, due to the trauma and your lack of consciousness. Please, sit back, you're hooked up to several machines at the moment."

"Who are you?"

"I'm Kerri, the label hired me on as your private nurse. I'm here to get you whatever you need."

"Good, what I need is my stuff. I'm not staying in this cowpoke hospital another second."

"*That* I can't do. What I can do is call your manager, Thomas Christy, and let you talk to him. He's staying in town and said to call him when you woke up."

"You do that then because I'm not having this bullshit."

Kerri nods and steps out of the room. I look around and push the call light. I'm in pain and need something. Fuck, my whole body aches. A moment later, a tall, dark, and handsome man in scrubs comes wandering in.

"Yes, can I help you?"

"Yes, I'm in pain. Can you give me something?"

"Let me see what they are giving you."

"He pulls up my chart on the computer against the wall and shakes his head. I can give you some Acetaminophen, but that is all."

"That's like a Tylenol, that shit ain't gonna cut it. Can't I have a Perc or something? I'm in a shit ton of pain here."

"Sorry, Miss Fontaine, but you came in on an Opioid overdose. The last thing we are going to do is give you more. Now, do you want the medication or no?"

"Fuck." I tilt my head back, my skin on fire. "Yes, I'll fucking take it. Just hurry the fuck up with it."

"Now, now, patience is a virtue, my dear."

"I ain't patient, and I ain't your fucking dear. Now do your damn job!"

∗ ∗ ∗

I'm lying here dying when Thomas shows the fuck up. "Hey, babe, tough break. You shouldn't have chased a handful of Dilaudid with a bottle of vodka."

"I had a long night. I was just trying to get some sleep."

"For the rest of the year? You don't take the Dilaudid to sleep. That's what the Ambien was for, but you had that in you too, on top of some Excedrin Migraine, Topamax, *and* Abilify. Were you trying to kick it?"

I look at him wildly. "Why the fuck would I do that? I'm the lead singer of the hottest southern rock band in the country!" It hurts to scream, but I'm pissed. "No, I was fucking tired. I busted my ass in the studio all day by myself and wanted to actually sleep for a fucking change!

He just shakes his head. "We've had a talk, the band and me, and we can't keep doing this with you. You've got one last shot or you're done. You hear me? You're going back to rehab."

"Oh, fuck that." I roll over, my whole body rejecting that idea.

"Then you're gone. Brent will have Marissa take over and you will never sing again."

I stare at him. Would he actually do it? I know Brent would love to see me gone. Fallen Angels was and is my lifeline. It's kept me from going completely insane. I need it more than the coke, or the pills, or the sex.

"Decide Angelica because once I leave here, there will be no going back… No changing minds and no renegotiating."

I swallow. "I don't wanna be gone..." I whisper, choking on the words. "I'll go back into rehab."

"Fine, we will be hiring you a specialized bodyguard and support specialist. He or she will help you to maintain your home and your sobriety once you get out. They will live with you and you will pay them to make your life better. You will agree to this or again, you are gone."

I nod my head. "Yes."

"Then it's agreed. We will draw up the contracts and have you transferred to the rehab facility in the next few days."

"Okay." I sniff as Thomas leaves the room. How the fuck am I going to get through another stint in rehab without my parents getting wind? The last thing I need is them beating down my door, upheaving my past, and bringing secrets to light that need to stay in the darkness.

2

MAVERICK

ELEVEN IN THE FUCKING MORNING AND I'M sitting in the waiting room at Imogen Records. I've heard a lot of good things from this label, not that I would ever have any use for it. So not my field of expertise. They could probably do for a new receptionist because since I walked in, she's been too busy chatting up her girlfriend on the phone and filing her perfectly manicured nails.

"Mister Donovan, Mister Christy will see you now," the receptionist says, still not paying any attention to the world around her.

I stand, stopping at the desk. "Which door?" I ask, waiting a few seconds and getting no answer. I clear my throat and ask again.

"Very sorry, I didn't see you there. It's the last door on the left." The receptionist throws me a bitchy smile.

I head off the way she said, in search of Mister Christy and my interview. I stop at the door where I see two men standing and talking. The taller man looks to be about the same height as me, red headed, and rockstar to the core. His tats and piercings yell that he's in the band.

I'm going to assume, by the looks, he's always in the background, but he likes it that way. He's got a secret he doesn't want anyone to know. The smaller guy, dark headed and dressed in a suit, must be the manager. He's looking rough around the edges, but we all are a little. With a knock on the door, they look in my direction.

"Mister Donovan, come on in and grab a seat. This is Ringo, he's representing Fallen Angels," Mister Christy says.

I walk over to Mister Christy and shake his hand. "Thank you for taking the time to meet with me," I say, turning to who I assume is Ringo. "Nice to meet you, I'm Maverick."

As soon as Ringo takes my hand, I see another guy walking up behind him and he's built like a Mack truck.

"This is Steve, he's the drummer." Ringo points over his shoulder.

I move around him to shake Steve's hand. "Nice to meet you, Steve."

"Sup, bro." Steve shakes my hand a bit firmly, but it's just a man marking his territory sort of thing.

"Now that all that's settled, how about we get down to business?" Christy asks, pointing to seats. I'm to the right, with Ringo in the middle, and Steve on the left. "You come highly recommended by one of the bigwigs here at Imogen. Says you did him a solid a couple years ago."

"Charlie Wilson? Yeah, he needed some help and I just happened to be around to lend a hand."

"Yes."

"What exactly did you help *with*?" Ringo asks. He's

a bit on the standoffish side.

"I'm sorry, I can't answer that. Charlie is a private man."

Steve clears his throat "Well, can you tell us what you can do for us?"

"Of course. I've worked in multiple private rehabilitation centers and had a few private home jobs. I'm certified as a counselor, physical fitness trainer, nutritionist, and physician's assistant."

Ringo whistles, looking at Steve and Christy. "How old are you?"

"That's very ambitious of you," Christy says.

"Not that it's relevant, but I'll be twenty-seven in June. AP classes all four years of high school." The look on Ringo's face lets me know he's calculating my age with all the schooling it takes for each degree. "By the look on your face, you're trying to figure out how I finished in eight years with all four degrees," I say to Ringo before looking at Steve. "Just as you're supposed to be here to make sure your friend's voice is heard," I remark before finally turning my attention back to Christy. "And you know exactly what I've done, or you wouldn't have set this interview."

"You're right, I am here to make sure her voice is heard. She's a special girl and needs to be handled a certain way. From the looks of you, you might last a month," Steve comments.

"I don't know about that, Steve. He might be just what she needs," Ringo observes, rolling his shoulders. He seems so tense that said shoulders are tighter than my shoe laces. "Why are you so good at what it is you do?" he asks me.

"I grew up in New Port, Tennessee. If you don't know about the area, it's not the best town to grow up in. To make matters worse, I was the only white kid on the block besides my twin sister. Everyone I knew was on some form of something or would drink themselves stupid. After watching my dad die of an overdose when I was twelve, I decided I'd be the one to get out and do what was needed to make the world better, help the ones that needed it because in their minds, they can't help themselves. They don't see it as they are doing anything wrong. They think one joint and that's it. One line, one drink, one of whatever their drug or drugs of choice may be. However, that one may just be the difference between life and death. The only reason I can help is because I was raised around it."

Each one of these guys is looking at the other and back at me. Ringo's pretty easy to tell as is Christy. Steve, on the other hand, is trying to hide behind his tough man persona.

Christy looks at me. "Well, the girl's got some rehab to go through first, but you're gonna have to go through her home. Do you have a problem doing that?"

"Not as long as you don't mind that while I do, I remove anything that could set her back in her recovery. Things like books, movies, stuff that may remind her of hard times. Does she have a fitness area in her home, or will that be something I need to look into setting up for her?"

"To tell you the truth, I'm not aware. I've never been in her home," Christy responds.

"She doesn't have equipment or anything like that; she has a dance room. She does yoga and Pilates. She used to run," Steve states.

"Then I need to set up a full gym. It helps the body work out the problems. Will I be staying in her home with her all the time?"

"Yes, she has a cottage on the premises that you will be living in," Christy says.

"We'll be in two different houses? Um, does she have an extra room in hers? It's better for me to be close at all times in case she wakes in the middle of the night or anything."

"That can be arranged. She does have other rooms in the house. Now, there was another matter. You seem to be a sturdy fellow. Her bodyguard needs to be replaced. Could you take on that role as well, or will we need to hire on another person?"

"Sir, to be honest, there will need to be two people there at all times in case she becomes erratic or unstable. If she is the type that doesn't like people, we'll have to make it work with just one. I can do the job alone with no problem, I just want what's best for the client."

"She's easier to handle in a one on one situation. She doesn't trust easily. If she feels cornered, you're not going to get anywhere with her," Steve offers. He seems to know her best. Leads me to wonder if there was an intimate relationship.

"In that case, yes, I'll be better off alone and I'd most definitely need to be in the house, close to her at all times. Do you have an idea of when she will be coming home?"

"At least a month. Her rehab is going to take twenty-eight days," Christy says.

"Tell him," Steve barks.

"Tell me what?"

"That she isn't exactly doing this out of her own free will. This is a last shot for her," Christy states.

I can't hold my laughter in. "Do you think any of them do this out of their own free will?"

"There will be a lot of resistance because you're a

man."

"Into chicks, got it. Even better because dating is off the table."

3

ANGELICA

"PLACE ALL OF YOUR BELONGINGS IN THE bag," the woman at the desk instructs me as Thomas gently rubs my back. The fuck is acting like he gives a shit about how I feel about all of this when all he really cares about is how it looks for him and the rest of the Imogen cronies. They've tucked me away at some rehab facility in the hills that I've never heard of before. Sacred Hours Guiding Light. Sounds more like a fucking commune or a cult than a rehab, but I've agreed to it and can't back out now. They take all my credit cards, jewelry, and makeup. The hospital took my medications while I was unconscious. I've got the itch already. They pumped me full of some kind of shit that was supposed to detox me, but I don't think it did a very good job because I can feel it coming. Mother fuck, what I wouldn't give for a line right now, or a good stiff drink, hell, anything but this blinding sobriety. I feel like my skin is crawling with ants all over.

"This will be good for you," Thomas says as the orderlies come for me. "This place will be good for you."

"I hate you," I sneer as one puts out his hands for me to follow and the other hands me a pair of white scrubs and some blankets.

"Right this way, Miss Fontaine, and we'll get you settled in," the second one says. "My name is Lenny and I'll be on most afternoons if you need something. This is Francis, he's on mornings on your wing."

I nod, following. "I'm not here to make friends. I'm just gonna do my time and get the fuck out of here."

"With that attitude, you're not going home anytime soon." Lenny shakes his head.

"Screw that, twenty-eight days and I'm done."

"Eh, it's a suggestion, not mandatory. If you've not made progress, they will keep you."

"Fuck that."

"It works if you work it," Francis repeats the AA mantra. I've heard it a thousand times before.

"And yet here I am."

We walk through a common area where others are talking and watching TV. Some are playing games and some, well, they are obviously riding the night train. So, they give out meds here. I wonder how I can get on that bandwagon. A little Trazodone, maybe some Xanax cocktails. Those are always a good time for me. Then we turn down a hallway and the screaming starts. I know this hall. Every rehab has one, they just don't advertise it in the brochures. It's the detox wing. They drop you in a room with a bed and a toilet for a week to ten days and let you ride it out. I'm already five days in, but under medical supervision, now the hard detox is going to start. The chills, the body cramping, the vomiting. God, I don't wanna go through it. I hesitate and the orderlies' demeanor flips like a switch as they grab me by the arms.

"No, please!" I scream, dragging my feet, but they just lift me up and take me to a room where two female orderlies are waiting. I'm stripped and made to put on the scrubs before finally, I'm left crying and alone.

* * *

The night is horrible. They bring me food, but I can't keep it down, even water is difficult. Everything tastes like ash and bile. I'm barely able to control my bowels. This… This is why I stayed high. This is why it was easier to always be on something. Coming off of it all, cold turkey like this, it's cruel, it is a punishment. I know I am a cunt, I know I am a vengeful, hurtful person, but this, this is not Karma, this is just wrong.

I'm curled up on the floor in the bathroom, wrapped around the toilet and sleeping in spurts. I only know morning has come by the sound of the breakfast tray being delivered. The smell of the eggs hits me and I hurl again. How can they torture me so noticeably and not feel bad? I feel the anger rise up in me and am up, racing on feet that feel like they are on fire toward the tray. No utensils, just the paper plate and the plastic tray and lid. I take the lid and smash it into the wall, then take the tray and smash it over and over again into the door. The orderlies come down the hall and I'm sure they have something for me, some sedative, something to chill me out.

The door opens and they have something all right, a jacket with straps and buckles. I'm grabbed and forced into it as they drag me out of the room and down the hallway to the nice small room with the padded walls.

4.

MAVERICK

MOVE IN DAY. For some, move in day is a cool thing, for me and this job, it's a ninety-day probationary period. If they like the job I do, then I stay on and if not, I'm gone. I've packed up all the necessities and Lucille. Lucille is my mouthy calico. I've had her two years now. She was six weeks old when I found her stuck up behind my truck tire, couldn't leave her there, so I took her home.

I've got all my bills and rent paid up for the next ninety days. Now, there's nothing left but locking up and heading out.

The drive from my apartment to Angelica's house takes all of an hour. Pulling up, it's gated which is good, means I can keep out the riff raff. I hit the pin number and the gate opens. I finish the drive up to the house and stop when I see Christy. The house is huge.

"Hey," I say, getting out of the truck.

"Hello, Donovan. These are the keys to the house. The fridge is stocked and here's our company credit card. Anything you need, you can use this for it. It's all tallied up. It's just gonna be you in the house. There are some landscapers and those that tend to the horses. They never come in the house, but you may see them on the property."

"Sounds good. I'll take today to get moved in and adjusted. It'll take me a good week to two weeks to get the house gutted and ready for her to come home. I'm going to put cameras up on the inside... Just so you are aware."

"Not in her private spaces, though, right?"

"Her bedroom is completely off limits, but there will be one in the hall at her door. Everywhere else in the house is fair game. It's how I keep an eye on her without her feeling strangled."

"That's fine. As long as it doesn't end up on YouTube, I don't care what you do."

"I would never. I do need to know if you need a copy of the tapes or if somebody else does. I track everything, I just need to know who they go to."

"Unless you feel something needs to be seen by us, just destroy them when you're done."

"Will do. Thanks again for giving me the job."

"Let's hope you can keep our girl on the straight and narrow. You have yourself a good day," Christy says as he's walking to his car, getting in, and leaving.

After Christy is gone, I pull Lucille out of the truck and bring her inside. The first thing I see as I walk through the door is a black light aquarium with an albino eel. That isn't normal. Lucille is off exploring as I bring myself into the entryway.

Boxes, bags, and everything in the house and in the room that is two doors away from what looks to be Angelica's room, I grab my tablet so I can make notes on my walk through. The living room is big and spacious.

Needs more of a home feeling. The kitchen is homier but doesn't appear to ever be used. I check the cabinets, then the fridge and find everything has to go. Her room is done in black. The fitness room looks to have been used for social gatherings. There's a gym right off the workout room that will come in handy for Angelica. She has her own entertainment and game room.

The entire house has to be gutted and deep cleaned. I've got a long two weeks ahead of me. I begin the unpacking process after I've thoroughly searched and cleaned the room top to bottom. It takes me four hours to get the whole room done.

My list just from the walk-through is a start. I will need to make a trip to the store tomorrow. For tonight, I'm going over the two lists I have to make sure I'm not missing anything.

Things to talk with Angelica about
Aquarium, one fish?
Why she feels alone?
Does she know how to cook?
Lots of black. Lonely?

Stuff I need to order or go get
Cameras
Healthy Goods
Fitness Equipment
Cleaning Supplies

Not a lot here, but that will change as I work on each room.

5

ANGELICA

"WE APOLOGIZE FOR THE ROUGH START, Miss Fontaine," a woman says, handing me a towel. It's been four days and I have finally been allowed to shower since I've calmed down and become more complacent. Having the pain go away finally will do that to a girl. I wrap the towel around me and nod, forcing a smile.

"Who are you?" I ask.

"Doctor Miranda Peters. I'm one of the counselors here. I have been assigned to your case. I hope that I can aid in your recovery."

"Uh huh," I answer. Another head shrinker whose sole purpose is going to be to try and get me to talk about my past. Fuck that. "I'm not much for the feelings, Doc."

"We have to talk about the drugs, when it started, why you hit bottom when you did. It's important."

"Whatever. Can I get dressed now?"

She steps out of my way as I head for a fresh pair of white scrubs. They don't even give us undergarments.

17

I'm glad I don't have really big tits or I'd be in trouble. Sheesh.

"We have a group session after breakfast in the common room, we do hope you'll join us," Dr. Peters says before walking out. I finish getting dressed and come out of the shower room to find Lenny waiting.

"All fresh and clean? Ready to see your new digs?"

"I suppose." I gesture for him to lead on oh so enthusiastically.

We walk down the hall and take an elevator to the second floor and here he shows me to a single room with a private bathroom and shower that they were just finishing cleaning. "Seriously, I had to shower with supervision when a few minutes wait would have lent me a long hot shower?" I spit.

"It wasn't ready yet, and they do that... Tear you down. You gotta come off that horse."

"Yeah, whatever." I roll my eyes and he leaves me to the room. It's not the Ritz-Carlton, that's for sure, but at least they didn't lock me in this time.

✻ ✻ ✻

"You think cause you gots a bit of fuckin' money, you entitled to better?" A large, dark skinned woman leans toward me as I attempt to sit in the stupid fucking group. I couldn't help but complain that with how much I knew I was dropping on this place, they could at least feed us better than the slop that they were slinging. Apparently, she took offense.

"Actually, that's exactly what I'm saying. I bust my ass so I can have better and I fucking expect it too," I shout back.

"Denise, Angelica, ladies, please." Dr. Peters tries to

calm us. Good fucking luck there. I snap my attention to her.

"See, this is why I don't do group sessions, Doc. Some poor piece of nothing takes offense too fucking fast and I'm left defending my ass from a shiv later tonight. Thank a fucking lot." I stand up and go to walk away, but Lenny is there to stop me.

"Sit," he demands and I don't like it one bit.

"You sit, I ain't your fucking bitch, you don't command me." I go to walk by him and he grabs me. This time, I'm ready and nail him in the balls. He drops and I run. Don't know where I'm running to, but I figure my room's a good start.

I just about make it when Francis heads me off and whips me around. He drags me down the hall and into an office, dropping me into a chair, keeping his hand on my shoulder so I don't get up. I sulk down, pulling up my feet.

"Fuckers," I grind out which makes him chuckle.

"You've got plenty of spirit. That's good, now use it to get better."

"Suck my clit."

He bends down to my ear. "Is that an invitation?" he whispers, sending an uncomfortable chill up my spine just as the door opens and he straightens up.

"Francis, you can go," Dr. Peters orders as she comes around the desk and drops her hands exhaustedly on the table before her. "You are trying to do all you can to sabotage yourself. Why?"

"I just want out of this place and that ni- *Woman* came at me. I was trying to advocate for my health, hell, for everyone's health. The food is terrible. We need more leafy greens and red meats, fish and not the kind that comes as a stick. Not fried egg sandwiches and piles of greasy pan baked bacon and sausages."

"It's Fried Friday, the only day of the week they are allowed those types of foods, Angelica. We do all the healthy foods, juices, and smoothies. We have yoga and a pool too. You just haven't earned those privileges because you're too busy being a brat."

"Aren't you supposed to be like using I statements and shit, not being accusatory and what not?"

"Would that work with you?" She raises an eye at me.

"Fuck no, it would piss me right the fuck off."

"So, why would I want to do that, when what I want is for you to talk to me?"

I stare at her. The tactic isn't new, but it has been a while since anyone tried it while I'm completely sober for it. "I'm not talking about my family and my childhood, it's irrelevant now. I have no contact with them anymore."

"Fine. Let's talk about the bipolar, that's what you were self-medicating, correct?"

I nod. "They diagnosed it when I was twenty. I never told the label because I was afraid they wouldn't take us on if they knew. I know people, though, so getting meds has never been hard."

"And these people, were they monitoring you? Watching for side effects, keeping track of your episodes?"

I laugh. *"Yeah, okay,"* I answer sarcastically. "I've never been one to really get down, I'm not the type. My lows have always been like most people's version of normal. But my ups, they can be… Well, I'm a fucking Rockstar! I get to bleed music for a living!" I squeal. "I get my outlet there. It's helped me through just about every fucked thing I have had to deal with."

"When you say every fucked thing? You refer to the emancipation at fifteen?"

"I said I didn't wanna talk about that."

Doc Peters nods. "Yes, perhaps, but it was just after the emancipation that the issues with the drugs and alcohol became public and you were in the tabloids for the first time."

"If you wanna split hairs, but it wasn't all a neat little bow. It's a sloppy, fucked up situation and I'm not ready to share it with you or anybody else." I cross my arms and pull up my knees again. "Can I go back to my room now?"

Doc Peters nods and I get up, leaving her office. She wants my secrets. I can't give them to her. They are mine and they need to stay buried or I'll never be able to do this.

* * *

This place... It's not cushy, it's not a spa, but it has a few niceties, the pool, for instance, and a gift shop where I am allowed to add some commissary items to my tab, like tampons that I, of course, needed last week and chocolate. The endorphin rush of that legal drug is so satisfying after nearly three weeks of nothing. They've put me back on meds for the bipolar. A low dose of Trazodone at night to sleep and Lithium with a Depakote chaser.

It makes me a little fuzzy, not high, but I just feel like I'm not totally at top speed. The good news is I'm functioning at the low doses and they are happy with my progress, so I guess it's a win. I've got one of my final appointments with the Doc today, but I'm not sure I'm ready for it yet. She wants to talk about the night I

OD'd. The problem is I don't remember much of it.

I'm out of the pool by lunch time and head out to the cafeteria. I keep to myself. Since that first week, I've pretty much had to. Denise made a pariah out of me. It's good though, better than word get out of just who I am. I spotted an orderly with a camera last week and reported him. Haven't seen him since. I have my roast beef and roasted potatoes with broccoli and then head up for a quick shower before my appointment. To my surprise, I find my room isn't empty.

I'm face to face with Steve, my drummer, and Doc Peters. I hesitate, why is Steve here? Has the band decided I'm out? Is this him pulling the plug before I'm even done?

"I- Steve? What are you...?"

"The Doc reached out... You haven't been talking and she was looking for insight."

"You didn't?"

He drops his head. "Needed telling, Queenie. Please understand, it's for your own good." Steve is standing there, all six feet four inches of tattooed and pierced muscles of him and I don't give a shit. I fly at him, punching and banging on that monkey chest of his.

"Yo-you had no fucking right! It wasn't yours to tell.... You son of a bitch!" Hard tears are streaming down my face as he grabs me and hugs me, letting me pound on his back as my knees buckle and I start to drop, but he's so big and strong, I'm held in place by his hold.

Steve strokes my short, shaggy blonde bob and shushes me, picking me up and sitting me down on the bed. He keeps me in his arms, cradling me up like one of his little girls. "It's okay, Queenie."

"Angelica, Steve here has only explained the root of

your use where you couldn't. It is a pivotal thing to address. This kind of thing… I would like you to continue to come see me once you leave here. I have a private practice in Clark County. I'm sure your insurance will be fine. I would hate to see you have to start over with a new psychiatrist, especially at such a major breakthrough moment for you."

I cling to Steve. As much as I hate him right now, I need him, need his strength to listen to the Doc. He'd told one of my biggest secrets, but how much had he told her? Was it just the highlight reel or had he given her the whole picture? It was up to me to suss it out now.

"So now you know about my stepfather and how my mother chose him over me," I sniff, wiping at my face, "which led to my downward spiral and my needing to get out of that house, but did Steve tell you about Angela too?"

6

MAVERICK

MY LAST RUN-THROUGH OF THE HOUSE went as well as expected. It will be much different once Angelica gets home. It's always different when the client gets here and sees that their house has been gutted and redone to suit their needs. There is nothing in this house except stuff that is good for her, or anyone for that matter.

The plan for when Angelica gets home is to sit her down and go over the new schedule, meal plans, and counseling sessions. We've got lots of work to do in the first thirty days as it's always the hardest. I've fired all her staff except the couple who work with the horses and the landscapers.

Lucille's been fed and I'm checking the clock because Angelica is coming home today. It's three now and there is no sign of her. I check over the files and charts I have sitting on the counter, ready for Angelica.

❊ ❊ ❊

Five in the evening and the door finally opens and shuts then I hear, "Marko, make me a pineapple smoothie." I'm going to assume this order is coming from Angelica.

I sit up straighter at the counter and get ready for the first encounter with Angelica. She turns the corner and I get a good look at her. She's a bit small, looks like she hasn't eaten a proper meal in ages. She doesn't look as though she's just gotten out of rehab either. Freshly done nails, hair is cut and styled, and I'm betting she's had a wax with the way she's walking in those heels.

"Sorry, no Marko here," I say, watching her closely.

She looks me from top to bottom before clicking her teeth and saying flatly, "*The Manny?*"

I get off the stool and walk toward her "You can call me that, but I'd prefer Maverick. I'm going to take it that you are Angelica," I respond, putting out my hand for her to shake.

Angelica smirks and shakes my hand. "Maverick? They must have had a field day with you in the schoolyard. Your mommy into Tom Cruise films?" she asks, slipping her hand from mine.

With a smile, I say, "Actually, I was named after a real person. A 17-year old named Samuel Maverick was killed in the Boston Massacre on March 5, 1770. In case you don't know, this was the trigger event for the American Revolutionary War. Maverick Square in Boston is named for him."

"Ya learn something new every day. Where's Marko?"

"He's not here and neither is Becca. They're not coming back either. If you'd have a seat over here at the counter for me, we can get started."

"I'm not going to sit nowhere till I get something in my stomach. I've not eaten anything all fucking day."

"Of course, that's fine. I've prepped enough meals for two weeks. After the two weeks, we will revisit your diet. I had planned chicken, but I have steak in here as well. Which would you like?"

She clicks her jaw, walking passed and looking in the refrigerator. Angelica grabs an apple and says, "I'm good," before walking off.

I walk behind her and just as we get to the entryway, she lets out a blood-curdling scream. She turns to see me and I'm not sure her feet even touch the floor as she climbs up me and clings to my back. "What is wrong with you?"

"What is that and what's it doing in my house?" Angelica shouts in my ear.

"Calm down, it's Lucille, my calico. You two should get along great. She's as mouthy as you already seem to be."

"Again… What is it doing in my house? Why is it messing with my stuff?"

"I live here, meaning so does Lucille. Do you have something in there you shouldn't?" I set her down before walking over to where Lucille is sniffing at Angelica's stuff and gathering it in my arms.

"You just keep that evil thing away from me. Put it on a leash or something. Put a bigger bell on it."

"She isn't evil and now I'm thinking she will be a part of your recovery. She also isn't a dog, so a leash isn't needed. As for her bell, it's just fine," I say to Angelica then look down at the pussy at my feet. "Lucille, bed, go," I say sternly and she goes off through the house.

Angelica shivers from head to toe. "Evil things."

"Now, if you'll follow me back to the kitchen, we have some things to go over before we can retire for the evening."

"Whatever, just fucking walk." She throws out her hand.

I walk back the way we just came and pull out a stool for her to sit. Angelica sits and I take the one I was sitting in a few minutes before. The seating puts us across from one another. I set her stuff down beside me and prepare for the battle I know is coming. "As you've already seen, not everything you'd normally have is still here. I gutted the house. There are no drugs, alcohol of any kind, caffeine, nor sugar. From here on out, you are going to be doing a lot of things I'm sure you haven't done in a long time. Luxuries such as getting your nails done, hair cut, or the wax you got won't be happening unless you earn them back." I lift my hand as she goes to speak. "I know it's in your nature to interrupt, but please, do me the courtesy of letting me finish what I'm saying as I will do with you." I jump back right into what I was saying, "Television is a reward. You earn rewards by doing everything that is needed of you. Counseling is a must as is learning how to take care of yourself without help. There's more, but I think I should let you speak before you explode."

Angelica's tapping her nails against the counter. "I don't know who the fuck you think you are and I don't give a shit that Imogen has hired you, but if you think you can dictate what I can or can't do to my body, you've got another fucking think coming. As for all the other bullshit, you wasted a hell of a lot of time because I could care less. The TVs, I don't watch them. They are background noise, but something tells me you are going to provide plenty of that."

"Tell me something. Why do you think I was hired?" I ask her.

"You're here to babysit. To make sure I stay sober, so the company doesn't lose any more money. Also, so I can go back on tour."

I smile and nod. "Thoughts are good, but I'm not just some, how was it you put it…" I pause, "…*Manny*. I'm trained, certified, and have degrees in every field I've wanted to work in. They all just happen to matter in your case. I'm not here to babysit you as you so nicely put it. I'm here to help you with your recovery."

"Yeah, well, right now, all I'm looking to recover is my bed. Everything else you need to know is in the fucking file. Now, if you would kindly give me my bag, I've got stuff for you."

"I'm sorry, but as of now, nothing is personal, so I can't give you back your bag till I've gone through it. I'm sure you haven't noticed yet, but there are cameras everywhere inside except your bedroom and bathroom. These first thirty days won't be easy, but I assure you, it gets easier. I'm of the mind that you must earn my trust and respect. You can go to bed anytime you feel tonight, but starting tomorrow, I will knock on your door between six and six-thirty. I expect you to be in here by seven to start your day."

"Well, you might as well dump my whole God damned bag so I can take my pill and go to fucking bed. Can I have my tampons or do I need to earn those too?"

"Pills? For what? You can have your tampons, smart ass."

"Oh, I'm sorry, are you not up to speed? There's a hunky dory little file right there that will tell you everything you need to know. Along with my prescriptions, showing you everything in my bag is legal

28

and that I only have enough to last me forty-eight hours."

"How about this? You go ahead and take a shower and after I finish reading your file and looking over your medication list, I will bring whichever it is you need to you. If it's one to help you sleep, you shouldn't be taking it till nine or so either way. Is this something we can agree to or would you like to sit there as I read over your file?"

"I can do that."

I dump out her bag on the counter and hand her a tampon. "Great. I will knock on your door when I'm done."

Angelica snatches the tampon from my hand and walks away. My God, this girl is going to be a pain in my ass. I fix my tablet so it's a laptop and get busy reading over the file and taking notes.

7

ANGELICA

UGH! Fucking cocksucker. If I didn't want to keep my fucking band, I'd be smashing his fucking face in with a God damned fucking chair. Telling me what I can and can't do and when I can have a fucking bikini wax! Bringing that evil little thing into my house! Who the hell said he could bring a cat in! The guys are probably doing it to get back at me. They know I'm terrified of cats. The bastards.

My room is almost as I left it. The TV is missing from the wall as are the rest of my electronics, my laptop, and I'm guessing my computer in the office is probably gone too. He's going to cut me off. I bet I don't get my phone back tonight either. Whatever. I'll put up with him, but if he thinks he's gonna lay a hand on me, he better think again.

I head for my closet and find that he's been through my clothes! What the actual fuck? My belts are gone, my shoe laces are all gone, and my scarfs are missing too! Like I'd hang myself ever? I told them all I wasn't trying to off myself, for fuck's sake! I open my drawer, I need a little me time. Okay... Seriously, this guy's a fucking pervert on top of it all, he took my vibrators!

❀ ❀ ❀

Showered and still steaming, I slide into a pair of pink silk shorts and a matching button down with a black chemise underneath before slipping on my black fuzzy slippers and heading back out.

"Hey, Manny? You know, if you needed suggestions on how to get off, you could ask instead of experimenting with a girl's stuff? Some of that could hurt a beginner..." I shout as I'm walking through the house toward the kitchen. Then I hear it, the bell. I stop and turn to see the animal behind me. I pick up the pace, and so does the bell, till I'm running straight into the kitchen and smack at the Manny, knocking papers everywhere.

"My God, woman, do you ever settle down? The cat isn't going to eat you?"

"Yeah, then why is it following me? Hell, it chased me in here! Look at those beady yellow eyes! It's just waiting to pounce me!"

"She didn't chase you, she wanted you to pet her. She likes as much attention as you."

"She ran when I ran, that's a chase," I assert, climbing off the back of his stool and watching the cat closely.

"You're going to have to get used to her. She's not going anywhere, I'm not going anywhere, you're stuck with us."

"I have a healthy fear here. I was attacked by a feral cat as a child. I've got the scars to prove it," I say, lifting my top and showing him deep horizontal marks along my ribcage.

"And what did you do to the cat?"

"Walked by it." I push him on the stool, still keeping an eye on the cat. "It used to follow me all the time, then one day it started to chase me and chased me right up into the hallway where I lived and cornered me. So, now I don't like cats."

"Lucille, come here," he commands and like a good dog, the cat comes padding over. I take several steps back so that I'm around the counter again, away from the feline menace. I watch him as he picks up and cuddles the monster. "Come over here, she isn't going to bite, just come here."

I shake my head hard. "You're nuts if you think I'm going anywhere near that... That ... Cat."

"I promise she won't bite, she won't even growl or hiss."

"Yeah? Well, neither did the feral cat before it fucked me up."

"I promise this one's different."

I cross my arms over myself and swallow the lump in my throat. I'm shaking like a leaf. I can't move. I just stare at the cat.

He walks toward me and I back up, but he keeps coming until I'm stuck between the wall and him. Not a good idea.

"Back off, please," I beg, my voice shaking.

"Calm down. How about this? You have permission to hit me if she attacks, or growls, or hisses, or does anything aggressive."

I eye him. "If I hit you, it's not going to be pretty."

"Fine, but just take the chance."

I look at the color-blocked fur ball. I swear it looks like a little demon. "What do you want me to do?"

"I want you to pet her," he answers matter of factly.

I tentatively uncross my arms and cross them again, then start to put out my hand. The cat lifts its head and I jerk back. "Ah, what's it doing?"

"It wants you to pet it, just chill and pet," he urges me, lifting the animal to my semi opened hand.

I uncurl my fingers and they descend into soft, warm fur. It's not unpleasant, but I'm still not convinced it won't try and kill me. I pull away after a few seconds. "There, we good now?"

"For this evening."

"Can you back out of my personal space now?"

"Well, I mean, I suppose." He backs up and I step to the side. He thinks he's funny or smooth in some fashion. Boy, is he barking up the wrong tree. I'm off men, and if I was on them, I have rockstars to choose from.

"So, you've read my file, can I have my pills so I can have a cup of water and go?" I ask sarcastically.

"Actually, after reading your file, I'd prefer if you ate a better meal than what you ate."

"Oh, you mean considering the apple is somewhere in the foyer? Yeah, probably, but I'm not feeling chicken or steak, I'm not a big eater of things with a face."

"Well, that's going to have to change as it's a part of your diet."

"Wait, if I was a vegetarian, you'd make me eat meat? That's fucked up."

"But you're not vegetarian, are you?"

"By proxy, I am, I mostly eat chicken and fish. I'm not big into cow, anything for that matter. If you paid attention to my closet, you'd see not a twinge of real fur, or real leather either."

"Here's the thing, if you still eat fish and chicken,

then you're not a vegetarian, and in order to get a well-balanced diet, you need to eat it all. You may not like the meal plans, but until you can start helping with the meal plans, you eat what I make." He puts the cat down and follows me into the kitchen. He really does think he has me by the short and curlies, doesn't he? I open the fridge, looking for the chicken ones.

"I don't want to eat the red meat, you can eat those. Red meat tends to upset my stomach unless it's cooked certain ways or certain cuts and I'm pretty sure those aren't these. So, I'll eat the poultry and start eating the red meat when, like you said, I help with the food, which will be whenever I suppose."

"You don't know which red meats are in there. You also don't know which cuts are there, so if you want the chicken tonight, eat the chicken. As for the food plan, it's my way for the next two weeks. There is nothing in this house to eat or drink that isn't healthy for you."

"Whatever, if I wind up sick from your meal plan, you can hold my fucking hair while I puke on your tennis shoes."

8

MAVERICK

DAY ONE DOWN AND IF I WERE THE TYPE TO drink, I'd sure as hell need one about now. Angelica is more fucked in the head than anyone would realize. It's six in the morning and I'm already showered, dressed, and getting ready to knock on Angelica's door.

"Breakfast in forty-five minutes," I say while knocking, then head to the kitchen and get started for the day.

I get to the kitchen and get breakfast going. Today we are having oatmeal, baked in apples with cheese and eggs in ham cups. It will get her started off right and last 'till one. Angelica should be able to get plenty done by the time lunch rolls around.

Just as I finish getting breakfast on the counter, Angelica comes around the corner wearing Capris, a T-shirt, and her fuzzy bunny slippers. Those just won't do, not with her work.

"Have a seat. After breakfast, we will get started on your list for today. Everything on the list is color coded by times. We will get to that in a bit. Let's eat."

Angelica shrugs her shoulders as she sits down and begins eating. I watch her a few minutes before I pray quietly to myself. "Thank you for this food you've blessed us with. Thank you for the job you have so graciously made sure I have. Thank you for blessing Angelica and me with this beautiful day. In His holy name, Amen."

I look up to see that Angelica has stopped eating and is just staring at me. "Is there something wrong with your meal?"

"No, I just didn't realize you were one of those."

"One of whom?"

"The religious types. That's all."

"Just because I'm all put together and have degrees, doesn't mean I haven't seen things that would make some people's skin crawl. I wasn't raised in church, but I've been reading the Bible since I learned to read. I wouldn't say I'm the religious type either, but I believe there's a God and he makes sure I'm taken care of."

"Okay. Can you pass the pepper, please?" Angelica asks. I slide the pepper over to her and pick up my fork to begin eating.

We finish up breakfast and I show her the new chart. There is a different one for each day. This is Friday, so her list for today isn't horrible, but she won't like it either.

"Angelica, as you can see here, from eight till one, you clean the rooms set for whichever day it is. In this case, you have the living room, sauna, and the barbecue. We will have lunch at one, then you will move to the afternoon portion of your day. At this time, you can tend to your horses, or we can do counseling. There's also journals, dishes, and gym time, basketball or tennis. It's best if you get the cleaning done before lunch so that we can get the physical fitness and counseling out of the way before dinner. There also may be some days when you just want quiet time. There's a box labeled for each day and games if you'd like that as well. I'm sure you have something to say. The floor is now yours."

"I- I don't know where Becca kept everything and I'm sure you replaced it with organic crap. So just point me in the right direction and I'll get started."

"Everything you need is in your utility room. Do you happen to know which you'd like to do today for your physical fitness?"

"Well, the first question is… Can I at least have the shoe laces back to one pair of tennis shoes?" Angelica tries to keep a straight face but ends up smiling.

"Promise not to hurt yourself? You have to understand that they weren't sure how you'd be when you got home."

"Considering I never was suicidal, I'd say it's safe to give me my shoelaces back. I understand if you have plans for my scarves and belts," she snarks, watching me.

"I've never been into the whips and chains shit. So, your scarves and belts are also fine." I smirk.

"Hmm."

"If you'll follow me, I'll give you that much back."

Angelica stands and we head off toward my room, just two doors down from her's. I stop in front of the door and pull my keys out of my pocket to unlock the door. I open the door and walk in, heading toward where I have her stuff packed. Turning, I look at her and say, "You may come in."

"Okay, just a firm believer in personal space," she says, looking around. I go back to my task at hand and hear, "Oh, my god, is that an HP Envy?" Angelica must be looking at my desktop.

"Yeah," I throw over my shoulder, pulling out a small tote that has all her scarves, belts, and shoe laces in it.

"Well, it's nice to see you're organized. Brent would love you."

"It's something you learn when keeping up with someone other than yourself. Brent? That's one of the guys in your band, right?"

"Yeah, way, *way* OCD. Like you can't touch his shit, or he'll literally explode. So, of course, I touch everything."

"Well, I'm not OCD. I just like things organized and in a place I can find them when needed. If you feel the need to touch, you can. I just prefer that you ask first."

"Eh, where's the fun in that? Is that mine?" Angelica asks, pointing to the small tote in my hands.

"Yes, as are the rest of the totes, but as I said before, you have to *earn* them," I tell her, handing her the tote.

"Thank you." Angelica takes it and walks herself out of my room with an extra shake to her ass.

If she weren't my client, I'd have trouble not watching the shake of her ass or the fact that she has just enough tits to fill my hands and mouth. I shake my head, turning on the computer screen so I can get some work done and watch her at the same time.

I make a call so that I can get someone out here to take Angelica's prescriptions and get them filled. As well as picking up a few odds and ends such as more tampons. With all that set, I grab *Lick* by Kylie Scott off the bookshelf and laugh. It wouldn't be so funny if it weren't considered a *Rockstar Romance.*

9

ANGELICA

HE TAKES ALL MY SHIT, NOW CHORES? Really? He put people out of work, good people, quite a few of them in fact. Becca and Marco were permanents, but they often hired temps to come in during the week to help them with the cleaning. Most of these rooms are at least a two if not a three-person job, and he wants me to do it alone?

For Christ's sake, I mean it's not that I'm *afraid* of a little hard work. I'd much rather be doing something than lounging around anyhow. I hate being idle, sitting still makes my mind race faster and drift to the past and I *never want that*. It's being idle that makes me wanna be high, makes me want that line of coke so badly because it's the thing that keeps me going twenty-four, seven. So long as I'm moving, I don't have to stop and think or even speak about myself or my life. I can just be the rockstar they all want. The *Drama Queen, Hell in Heels* as they've dubbed me in the tabloids on more than one occasion.

The publicity of my being seen all over Las Vegas

and California at the hottest clubs, shaking my ass and doing impromptu sing-offs is what sells records. As much as they don't want to admit it, they need me. Why else go through the trouble of sobering me up?

Back in my room, I change out of my Capris and T-shirt and toss on a pair of old ratty yoga pants and a sports bra, tying a button down over it. *Cleaning…* I'm not a slob, Becca never had to clean my personal space, I always took care of my room and bathroom, she was just responsible for keeping the rest of the house maintained while I was gone, and ready when I threw parties or got back. I lace up my Adidas' and head for the utility closet, passing by the Manny's room. He's just sitting there reading a book. I'll be damned if I'm going to be picking up after him. The fucker had better be cleaning up after himself. I may have to do this shit for now since it's mine, but I'll be fucking damned if I'm picking up after some man I ain't fucking. Hell, I wouldn't clean up after his ass if I was. Of course, from what I've seen so far, I'm suspecting he's as gay as the day is long, which is good. It means I don't have to worry about him checking me out or getting skeevy. I can be me and not have to act all appropriate.

I head for the sauna first. It's the smallest of the rooms to be done and one I've cleaned before, so I know I can bust it out fast. I think I may just use it later tonight, it'll be good for me, and make my shower feel even better after all the shit I'm gonna have to do.

✻ ✻ ✻

The sauna is done and finally, so is the living room. What a chore that was, those rugs are no joke, but I swept and vacuumed them just the same. I'm glad I don't put out a lot of knick knacks, so dusting was minimal. Though I did notice a stain on my couch that I about flipped over. Luckily, I found some baking soda in the closet and was able to get that shit out. I don't know what it was or where it came from, but I was not a happy cabbage. I've just finished the grill and it's only twelve-thirty. Fuck, it's hot out here. I look at my pool, nice cold water. Half an hour and he did say I need to exercise, right? I strip off my button down and my yoga pants, shoes, and am about to take off my panties when I remember the cameras. I hesitate a moment, then decide to have a little fun. I'm all sweaty anyhow, so I pull off the bra first, running my hands down my length, then hook my fingers into my panties and peel them off too before diving right into the cool, crystal clear water.

I'm on my second round of laps when I hear his voice through the water.

"What the hell are you doing?"

I'm at the farthest reach of the pool when I stop, coming up for air. "My taxes, what's it look like?"

"Alright, smart ass, out." He hooks his thumb at me.

"How's about this? You said I had to do some exercise anyhow, so let me get in my fifty laps while you make lunch and grab me a towel from the shelf over there." I point to the linen closet near him.

"How about not," he answers back sternly.

"Okay," I say, lifting myself out of the water and walking calmly around the length of the Olympic size pool. I pick up my clothes and smirk at him, heading back inside the house.

"Hey, Cupcake!" I hear him shout. "You may wanna get dressed, the house is gonna need a good mopping."

I stop and walk back to him, dropping my clothes to the floor and using my foot to clean up the mess all the way to my door.

After tossing on a new pair of yoga pants and a tank top, I head out to the kitchen, curious what he's made for lunch. As far as dinner goes, I'm hankering for something on the grill since I cleaned the damned thing. Might as well use it, I figure. I'm also wondering just what kind of trouble I'm in for my public display of nudity. I'm sure he's got something up his tailored sleeve.

I come into the kitchen and the house smells of peppers, onions, and garlic. My stomach instantly gurgles, I didn't realize how hungry I was until it hit my nose. I wander over to him as his back is turned and peek into the pan. It looks like chopped steaks sizzling up with cheese melting down on top.

"Cheesesteaks?" I ask, watching him toss a salad with strawberries. I love strawberries.

"Yeah, I figure you need some energy for what's still to come today."

"Oh?" I ask, reaching over him and snatching a strawberry from the counter, popping it into my lip-glossed mouth.

"I'd prefer it if you didn't touch the food, seeing as I have to eat it too," he snaps.

"Meow," I hiss at him with my nails scratching the air as I chuckle, walking over and grabbing a couple of plates and bowls from the cabinet since I didn't see any on the counter.

He watches me, then takes the dishes. "Thank you.

You can sit."

I shrug and roll my eyes, sitting down at the kitchen island.

He finishes up the lunch prep and sets the plate in front of me. I wait on him and his prayer ritual before cutting the sandwich in half and wrapping it in a napkin securely. Once it's set, I take that first bite.

"This is good," I say after a sip of water.

"Thank you," he answers shortly. Wow, I must have ruffled some feathers with my naked stroll and cleanup duty.

A smirk plays on my lips as we eat quietly. I take this time to really look at him. He's not hard on the eyes, dark hair, I think blue eyes, though his wire frame professor glasses are a distraction. He's not a total nerd. He's got tats, like serious inkage. From his right wrist, up under his T-shirt, is a grayscale piece that looks like twisted trees with dark red roses and storms brewing all around it, and around his left bicep looks like an hour glass with a flower of some kind. I also spied a tattered American flag done to look like it's wrapped and ripping through the flesh on his left calf. All of them are very well done. He doesn't appear to have anything pierced. Me, I'm the opposite. I just have the one tat, a strawberry dipped in chocolate on my bikini line, and the rest is piercings, ears, tongue, tits, and clit. You know, the essentials.

"I'm thinking barbecue for dinner. Is that doable with your meal plan?" I ask, taking the last bite of my cheesesteak.

"If that's what you prefer."

"Well, I just figure I cleaned it, so we should use it. You know the saying... Use it or lose it, and I haven't fired that thing up in months."

"If that's what you want, that's fine."

"*Okay*," I answer, policing my plate and taking it over to the sink to wash it along with my cup. "Since you wouldn't let me finish my laps, I decided I want to see my horses, is that good by you?"

"Of course, go ahead." He waves me off and I roll my shoulders, heading back to my room. I need my boots to ride.

10

MAVERICK

ANGELICA WENT TO SEE THE HORSES AND I get to breathe a sigh of relief. Not only is the girl pierced, but she has a fucking tattoo of a God damned strawberry dipped in chocolate on her bikini line. Took everything in me to keep my dick from standing at attention. Suppose I should have had a night out before the girl came home. Now that I'm thinking about it, I guess it's been since I was with my ex, but we've been split for a good four or five months now. She wanted something I wasn't prepared to give her.

I can't let what she pulled today go. It's time that I take action. I clean my dishes and the ones I cooked with, putting the leftovers in the fridge for snacks or whatever. I head off to my room, grabbing an empty tote and to Angelica's room I go. Popping the lid off the tote, I fill it with all her shoes except the one pair she was wearing earlier and the pair she has on now.

Before heading out of the room, I also grab the tote she got back today. Just as I get back to my room, the doorbell rings. I lock up my door and head off to the

45

front door. I open the door to find a boy, maybe nineteen or twenty, holding a brown bag. "Thank you, but how'd you get through the gate?"

"Oh, I scaled it."

"Are you fucking kidding me?" I jerk the bag from his hands. "Get the fuck out of here," I shout and slam the door. Jesus Christ! I'm going to have to put someone at the gate full fucking time.

**

I'm sitting out on the patio, enjoying the sun and finishing up the book I've been reading today. Angelica stops in front of me on her way in the house. She's bouncing from foot to foot. Apparently, the ride did nothing to help her wind down.

"So, do you want to do the gym first or this counseling thing? I figured I'd ask before I take a shower and change my clothes again because I'm not changing again since I'm assuming I have to do my own laundry." She laughs.

"Of course, you have to do your own laundry." I smile. "I'd say we do the physical portion first. The question is are we playing tennis, basketball, or working out in the gym?"

"Define work out because there's nothing in my gym."

I chuckle. "Gym it is. Grab your shoes and let me change. I'll meet you there." I refrain from calling her cupcake again because this is a working relationship. I need to watch my slips. Angelica skips off and I drop my head to the table before getting up.

Changed and walking into the gym, I spot Angelica with her hands on her hips, wearing her yoga pants with just a white sports bra with purple flowers on it. I mentally shake my head, walking over to the bar. I put my phone into the dock and get ready to hit shuffle when Angelica speaks up.

"So, I was thinking we could kill two birds with one giant stone."

"Okay?" I ask with my back still turned to her.

"I figure we could work out for an hour and you can just counsel me now, rather than, you know, working out in silence."

"It won't be silent. I've got music. Go ahead over to the mats and we will get you stretched out."

"It's just a thought."

I hit shuffle on my playlist and head over to the mats with Angelica.

"How ya want me?" Angelica asks and that's such a loaded question.

"Basic stretches."

I take a seat on the mat beside her and get us started on stretching our legs. She bends down, touching her toes and counting to ten. Only her chest is against the floor. Fuck me, she's limber.

Save a Horse by Big & Rich starts playing and Angelica bursts out in laughter. She sits up and begins dancing a little, doing lassoes over her head. I'd bet she could be a good cowgirl. I turn away from her, stretching my other leg.

"Do you need a little help?" Angelica snickers.

I jerk my head around to look at her. "I'm all right."

"Alright, it's just you wanted me to stretch and it looks like you could use a little help," she says, getting up and sitting back down in front of me.

She reaches for my hands. I give them to her and she pulls me toward her. I do the same with her and we go back and forth like this for about thirty seconds each. Every time she pulls me toward her, I'm so close to her that I can stick out my tongue and lick her. At the same time, when I'm pulling her toward me, I'm trying to think of everything except her mouth on my cock. *Baseballs, basketballs, footballs, lots of fucking balls. Fuck, her tongue would feel awesome on my balls.*

I change up positions just as the song changes again. *Ride* by Chase Rice starts playing and I feel myself blush from head to toe. I push her leg up, trying to stay far enough away so that my cock doesn't come in contact with her pussy.

Angelica lets out a little moan, "Push harder, it will go behind my head."

I clear my throat and push down on her deeper, my cock rubbing against her. I'll be damned if she isn't pierced there too. I know Angelica feels my cock against her as I move and she has to stifle a moan as her shoulders lift off the mat slightly. I let up on her left leg and go to work on the right. As soon as my cock touches her, the grip she has on my shoulders tightens.

Before I know it, Angelica's grip on me tightens to the point that I'm positive I'm bleeding and she spasms underneath me. The next thing I know, I can feel her nails in my scalp and I'm being pulled down. Before I can do anything, her tongue is in my mouth and I can feel the ring slide across my tongue. Angelica's left leg rolls over my hip and my cock stands at fast attention. I immediately push myself off Angelica and slide back so that I'm against the wall, watching her closely.

Angelica's chest is heaving, eyes wide and staring at me. "I'm so sorry. It's just- you were -and then I..." She laughs.

"You have nothing to be sorry about," I whisper. I'm fucked. I'm going to lose my God damned job and there's not a fucking thing I can do about it.

Angelica sits up, crossing her legs. "I'm confused. I thought you were gay."

"What gave you the impression that I was gay?" I ask.

"Have you meet *you*?"

"Well, I am me, so I'd supposed so."

"Add in the higher than normal organizational skills, the everything has to be in its place, the romance novels, the playlist..." She laughs. "But you kissed me back and um, that's still not going away," she remarks, pointing at my erection.

I run a hand through my hair and down my face. "I'm not gay, never been and pretty sure I never will be. As for everything else you can't always judge a book by its cover."

"That's very true." Angelica gets on her hands and knees and starts crawling toward me. "You know I can help with that."

"No, you have to stop. We can't do this. We won't do this," I say adamantly.

Angelica stops right in front of me with her hands on my ankles. "You obviously like me and I'm here and willing." She lifts herself up at the same time she tries to pull my legs down. "I already came, so it's *your turn*."

"Angelica! Stop! I can't and I won't," I say, picking her up and moving her out of the way so I can get up without hurting her.

She looks up at me and shrugs her shoulders. "I'm going to assume we're done then."

"Yeah, we are. If I can make other arrangements, I'll have somebody new here, come mornin'."

"Woah, wait. What? No! You have a contract. Ninety days. You've been paid for at least the first thirty, I know that. I've seen my bank statements and I had to sign the check."

"Angelica, I just fucked the contract. Do you really think I wouldn't have written a fucking check for every damn dime that was paid to me? I fucked up. I made an oath and fucked it all to fucking hell."

"Let's just roll it back. Okay? It was one little orgasm, one little kiss. I can forget about it if you can forget about it. Unless you have a live feed to Imogen, you can snip it out of the video."

"What do you not understand about me making an oath? I can't do this with you and it be ethical. I just can't."

"What part can't you do? What, the counseling? You haven't started. So, technically, you haven't done anything wrong. All the rest of it, well, there's nothing illegal there."

My legs give out on me and I drop to the floor. "I can't protect you anymore than I could her," I whisper as the first tear falls.

Angelica grabs me, hugging me. "What are you talking about?"

"Mariana. You and she have so much in common that it damn near kills me. I couldn't save her and now I can't help you either. I'm sorry, I fucked up. I will make sure they find you someone better than me."

"And if I refuse?"

"There's nothing to refuse. I can't work with you after everything that's gone on today."

"You still haven't told me why not."

"I've been wound up since you got out of the pool naked. It should never have bothered me. Not even two full fucking days and I messed up. Steve was right."

"Steve? As in, my drummer?"

"Yeah, he knew I wouldn't make it thirty days."

Angelica sighs and shakes her head. "And you're going to let him win?"

"There's nothing else I can do. I'm supposed to have control here and I shattered the same time you did, you just didn't know it."

"Give me the ninety days. We'll bring in Doc Peters to counsel me, but you- you'll do the rest. She already said she would."

I pull back and look her in the eyes. How does she think this will work? I have no control anymore. She just took it with one fucking orgasm, one fucking kiss.

"Please, something makes me want to trust you. And for me, that's hard," Angelica pleads.

"I can't do this or see you in that. I'm a man. This won't work."

"I'll do whatever you want. I'll be better. I'll wear a house coat. I mean you'll have to buy me one, but I'll wear it."

I bring my hand up so my palm is against her cheek. "You still don't understand. Two days and you've got me more flustered than someone I was with for two years. We crossed a line, we can't uncross it."

"We barely crossed it. Take a chance."

"Barely crossed? I just got you off without actually trying. Subconsciously, I think I knew what I was doing. Then I smelled you just before you kissed me. I can't undo *that*. I still haven't gone down because your smell is still in the air and the only thing I can picture is the look on your face as you were coming."

"Okay, so maybe we can't unring the bell, but why don't you take the time to get to know me? I think I'd like that because most people don't."

"Because every time I look at you, all I will be thinking about is burying my cock as deep inside you as

I can get."

"Please, you're my only hope. Christy told me if this doesn't work, then I'm done. As for your cock, I wouldn't be complaining."

"Angelica. I... I don't know," I stutter. "How can things stay the same after this?"

"It can't, you've made that clear, but I'm giving you power. I'm relinquishing it to you. What more do you want?"

"I'm going to hell," I say as I pull her toward me, our mouths crashing together as she climbs into my lap.

11

ANGELICA

FEELING HIS HARD COCK BENEATH ME AS I move up and down on him has me wet. Fuck, he's hard. He groans into my mouth and I break our heated kiss, sliding my hand down his firm chest, feeling defined abs under the T-shirt as I tease his waistband.

"Does little Maverick wanna play?" I ask with a grin, running my fingers through his hair with my other hand as he grabs my ass.

He licks his lips, watching my hand as my fingers rap on his stomach. "As much as I may want to, I can't."

"Really?" I ask, sliding my hand into his shorts and grasping him through his boxer briefs. "What's a little blow job between friends?"

"That's just it, we're not friends, we don't know one another," he argues.

I bite my lip, pulling my hand out of his shorts. "Okay, then you had better get to getting to know me, because this pussy," I grind down on him, "hasn't been serviced by a man in two and a half years."

"I'm pretty sure it was just serviced," he chuckles.

"Oh, you know what I mean." I take his hand and place it between my thighs. "You've already gotten me primed, but I guess it'll just have to be me and the shower head."

He lets out a needing groan and I can't help but laugh. "Unless you would like to clean up the mess you've made of me while I'm in there?"

"Are you trying to kill me?"

I stand up, "Nope, just letting you know that you have options," I answer, walking toward the exit. "I'll leave the door unlocked in case you have a change of heart."

✠ ✠ ✠

Freshly showered and mildly satiated, I come out of my bathroom and grab my pjs from a drawer. Sliding into the silky shorts and cami, I go looking for my slippers, finding they're not at the foot of the bed. I look under the bed and nothing. I check my closet and find all my shoes are gone! What the fuck? He took them? As punishment for earlier? My blood pressure rises. I don't care about the shoes, it's not like I'm going anywhere and need my heels, but those slippers? That's crossing a line we're about to be fighting over.

I head out to the kitchen and he's not there. I check the living room, *no Maverick*. Finally, I head to his room and try the knob... It's unlocked. I toss the door open and find, to my surprise, that he's standing there naked, drying his hair.

He looks at me then immediately wraps the towel around his waist. Before he can speak, I cut him off, my voice shaky, low, and slow.

"You. Took. My slippers." I try to swallow my rage.

"Please, give them back."

"You know I can't," he answers me, looking to the floor.

"Look, you can take anything else you want. Take my clothes, take my shower head, but please, please give me back those slippers," I plead. I can feel the tears crawling up inside me and I hate it

"Angelica, if I give them back to you then we can't do this," he says, still not looking at me.

I walk up to him, putting a hand on his chest. "You don't know what they mean to me, their value, they're a lifeline for me. Please, I'm begging you," I finish in a whisper. "They were a gift from my baby girl." On those words, the tears finally fall.

He pulls me against him. "You have a daughter? Why isn't that in your file?"

"Because I asked her to leave it out. Because I don't have her. Because she's not with me," I sob.

"That's not something that should have been left out."

"It's not something many know. It was about trust, about it getting out. I don't want anyone finding her." I sniff, holding him tighter.

"Angelica, you know if I give them back to you, then I have to quit and somebody else has to come in. I know you'll be mad at me, but there's nothing else I can do."

I pull away and push him back. "Fine, I understand. I'll just have to suck it up, I guess. I just... Please make sure that they're not just haphazardly tossed in some bin. They're old and tattered and I don't want them to fall apart."

"Do I look like the type that would just throw something haphazardly into a bin?"

I shake my head with a sniffle.

"All you have to do is do as I ask and not fight me," he says, watching me closely.

"I said I would try harder. This is me trying harder."

"Can we try and get through dinner without a fight?"

"Depends, do I still get barbecue?" I half-smile.

"If you want barbecue. I told you earlier you could have it."

"Okay. So, barbecue and maybe a movie after? You know, if we haven't killed each other or torn each other's clothes off first."

"He looks down at himself, then at me. "I'd have to get dressed first."

"That's fine, you can wear that to dinner. I'm not complaining in the least."

"Not happening."

"You afraid of the Vegas winds?" I smile. "I wouldn't be with what you're packing. But eh, you get dressed and I'll go get dinner prepped."

* * *

I scrounge through the fridge to see just what I'm tossing on the grill. I grab the chicken cutlets and asparagus as well as corn cobs and potatoes. I chop up the potatoes and season them up, tossing them along with the corn into foil packets. I take tomato sauce, molasses, brown sugar, and stone ground mustard, as well as the spices I need and get it all going in a sauce pan for my barbecue sauce. While that's simmering on the outdoor stove, I run inside and gather the spring greens for the salad and the peaches for the grill for dessert. I love fresh grilled fruit.

Just as I'm putting the chicken on the fire, I hear him come flip-flopping outside.

"You've been busy."

"I have." I smile, standing there barefoot and looking him up and down. He's in a pair of cargo shorts and a T-shirt. "We're having chicken with a version of my famous barbecue sauce, grilled asparagus, and roasted cob corn and potatoes with a nice spring mixed salad and Goddess dressing, and for dessert, grilled sliced peach halves in a brown sugar reduction."

"So, where do you need me?" he asks, looking around.

"Besides right behind me with a hand between my thighs, you mean?"

"I already told you, that's not gonna happen," he chuckles.

"Just have a seat and keep me company." I point to the patio table with my big grill fork.

He sits down and it's very quiet, so quiet I can hear my breathing between the sizzles of the chicken. "Are you not going to talk to me?"

He clears his throat. "I don't know how to turn it off."

I turn to him. "Turn what off?"

"The counselor."

I stop and walk over to him with a sigh and bend down to him. "Look at me and feel what you've been feeling. That should help, I think."

"I don't know how to do this as much as you don't know how to do being sober."

I push him back from the table and sit in his lap. "Okay, how's about this for starters? I'm Angelica Fontaine. And you're *Maverick...?*"

"Donovan," he answers me.

"Good. Now, I'm twenty-three, how old are you?" I ask, licking up his ear.

"Um, twenty-six," he answers with a heightened vocal tone.

I smile, leaning back. "There. See? Simple questions that we can both answer easily. Now, you try one."

He goes to speak and stops, then does it again. I drop my head to his shoulder. "Okay, if you can't turn it off, then just ask what you want to know, but be prepared to answer the same kind of question about you." I get off him and head back to the grill, the food needs my attention too.

"Why did you choose music?" he suddenly blurts out.

"You mean as a career?" I ask, turning the chicken.

"Well, yeah, you did that," he responds. I can tell he's searching for the right words and it's sweet.

"I got emancipated at fifteen and could always sing, so I panhandled for a while to make ends meet. Then, I got picked up by my first label. Sorta just fell into it all."

"And your band?"

"Rehab partners. Steve, Brent, and I met while I was coming off the coke the first time at twenty. My label had dropped me, but Imogen was sniffing around Brent and his twin brother, Kyle. When Brent realized who I was, it was like game on. What about you? I mean you're an ambitious chap, a PA degree, physical trainer, and counselor?"

"I didn't have the best upbringing. I... I grew up in New Port, Tennessee. It's not the best town to grow up in. I was the only white kid on the block besides my twin sister. Everywhere I looked or anyone I talked to was drugs or liquor. I watched my dad die of an overdose when I was twelve and decided then and there that I'd be the one to get out and do what was needed to make the world better. I wanted to help the ones that need it because in their minds, they can't help themselves. They don't see that they are doing anything wrong. You always think one joint and that's it. One line, one drink, one of whatever the drug or drugs of choice may be. However, that one may just be the difference between life and death. The only reason I can help is because I was raised around it, but I didn't succumb to it."

I pull the food from the grill and onto plates, thinking. The robotic way he answered doesn't sit well with me. I thought back to his breakdown in the gym. "Mariana, that was your sister?" I ask gently as I put the food in front of him and sit beside him. If he is going to get emotional again, I don't want to be far away. I know that I started this, not twenty-four hours ago, wanting to strangle this man, wanting to go full on WWE with a kitchen chair over his head, but there is something in the moment that shows me he can be human, be vulnerable, that has my momma bear instinct on high alert and now, all I want to do is hold him in my arms.

12

MAVERICK

ANGELICA'S PSYCHOANALYZING *ME*. She's trying to turn the tables on me when, minutes ago, she was sitting in my lap licking my ear. It's going to take every bit of my willpower to keep my cock down. She's asking about Mariana. I don't talk much about her. I don't like talking about her, brings up way too many feelings.

Angelica set the food down on the table, then took the seat beside me. I know I should say something, but I freeze and just stare at the table. I'm not the one who's supposed to be getting help, she is. So, why is it that I feel like if I step the wrong way, everything I've worked for is going to be over?

I feel Angelica's hand on my knee. "Maverick?"

I blink before looking up at her. "Huh?"

"You went away. I asked about your sister and you went away."

"Sorry," I say stiffly.

"It's okay, you don't have to talk about it. There are things I don't like to talk about either."

"You need to talk though, to someone. It's a key point to your sobriety."

"And tomorrow morning, we'll call Doc Peters and get her out here at least three times a week."

"I think you should still do the journal, but let her have it instead of me. You can use it as a good outlet."

"I can do that. I used to keep a journal on my computer, but I don't have that right now."

"You know I can't give it back yet."

"Just making a point that I used to catalog stuff. It's just a habit. Dreams, songs, poems… That kind of stuff."

"I'm sorry for being a dick and treating you the way I am. I'm doing what works. I know you think I'm being a horrible person, but I promise I'm not trying to be."

"You're just doing your job and we're probably going to fight tooth and nail over it. So, business during the day and party at night."

"Angelica, I think we need to set some boundaries. There are just certain things we can't do. Okay?" Angelica nods at me. "I'm not having sex with you. It's a serious commitment, one that you are nowhere close to being ready to make. In the gym, we stretch *separately*. Most importantly, you must *stay dressed*. That means actual clothes and not white sports bras. Agreed?"

Angelica smiles like the Cheshire cat and nods her head. "Yeah, I'll do better. When you say, 'no sex,' does that mean no contact at all? Cause I don't know that I can do that… Not kiss you again. As long as we keep our clothes on?"

"Cupcake, you are tryin' to kill a man. I'll give ya kissin', but if it starts to move further, I will get up and walk away."

"Okay."

✾ ✾ ✾

The rest of the evening and Saturday went off without any problems. Both nights I got a kiss on the cheek before Angelica went to bed. Today, I've pretty much left her to her own devices, only checking on her from time to time.

It's just about lunchtime when I hear Angelica screaming. I head off in the direction of the laundry room since the last time I saw her, she was gathering all her stuff up. I open the door, step in, and slide, busting my ass on the floor.

"What happened in here?"

"I... I... I..." she stutters, crying and trying not to laugh at the same time.

I reach up and grab her, pulling her down so she's sitting, wet and on the floor with me. "Now, quit crying, laughing, or whatever the hell it is you're doing, and tell me what happened."

"I just put my linens and stuff in the machine and then it went kaboom, soap and water everywhere. Ouch, my ass."

"I sorta figured out the soap and water thing when I hit the ground. You put everything from your bed in the washer together? Why would you do that?"

"Look how big it is. It all fit with a shove."

"Guess what?"

Angelica drops her head. "I need a bigger washing machine and a lot of towels?"

I place my forefinger and thumb on her chin so I can get her to look at me. "Besides that, you don't have any other pretty and comfy sheets and covers like this. You are going to the stiff shit till I can get you some here tomorrow."

"I'll sleep in one of the other rooms."

"What do you think is in the other rooms, Cupcake?"

"I forgot... So, what do you have on your bed."

"The stuff I brought from home." A smile starts to play at the side of Angelica's mouth as she crawls into my lap. "What are you doing?"

"Can I sleep with you?"

"We've talked about this."

"No, no, just sleep. You on one side of the bed, me on the other. You can put a pillow between us, the Wall of China, barb wire fence, whatever. Please?"

I drop my head to her shoulder in defeat. "Killing me."

Angelica picks up my head, giving me a peck on the lips. "You should probably get out of here. I need to clean this up. Unless you intend to help me?"

"No, ma'am. I've got to change then make lunch. After lunch, we can order you some new bedding."

"Ooh, shopping. Get out of here before I lose what little composure I have left."

"You have to get up first."

"But I'm comfortable," she says, wiggling.

"Not funny," I admonish.

Angelica grabs me by the ears, kissing me quickly before standing. I look her over from head to knees since that's where the soap hits her. She's a beautiful girl and she knows it. However, the drugs and drinking did a number on her.

I leave her and head straight for my bathroom. As soon as I get in there, I slip off my flip-flops and they are ruined. Son of a bitch. I jump in the shower, cleaning all the soap off me. With a towel around my waist, I go out to the bedroom to get some clothes. I look in my closet and all I see are jeans and cut off T-shirts. I let out a sling of profanities that is interrupted by a knock on the door. "Yeah?"

"You all right in there?"

I clear my throat. "Never better."

"Alright, well, I'm gonna go take a shower, then I'll come help you with lunch."

"Take all the time you need," I respond.

✤ ✤ ✤

The rest of the day was pretty mellow since we didn't do anything major, considering we have no washing machine now, thanks to Angelica. We got our shopping done after lunch, which included more clothes for me since I'm down to a couple pair of jeans, briefs, and cut off shirts, three new pairs of flip-flops to replace my ruined ones plus a couple for standby, her new bedding times two, and a new washer.

Now I'm standing in the bathroom, wearing my briefs and a cut off shirt. With Angelica in my bed, I'm left weighing the pros and cons of this situation.

Pro… She's covered from head to toe. Angelica is actually wearing cotton pajamas tonight instead of the silk shorts and tank she's normally in. Con… My imagination has already undressed her twice.

Fortunately, I had an extra set of sheets. Thank Christ! I'd have hated having her in my bed when the sheets needed washing. I know I'm standing here, avoiding going into the bedroom, when I hear a knock and turn to the door.

"Did you fall in?" I hear Angelica ask through the door.

"I'll be out in just a second."

"Don't forget my pill."

"I won't."

I throw some water on my face to try and calm myself a bit. I smell myself once more and triple my already doubled deodorant. This is going to be the longest night in history. Walking over to the door, I turn the knob, opening the door and shutting the light off. Angelica is sitting on the edge of the bed, waiting for me. Her eyes are all over the room.

"What are you looking for?"

"The cat."

"Lucille's in the bathroom. I'm sure she'll be in here anytime."

"Does she get on the bed?"

"Naturally."

"Maybe I should rethink this," Angelica groans.

"She's not going to hurt you."

"She's not going to attack my feet? Sit on my head?"

"No, but you will be in her spot, so she may wallow a little at you."

"Well, I can move to the middle. It is a big bed. Then I'd be invading your space which wouldn't be a good idea. I'll just stay here on the edge."

"You don't have to be in the middle or on the edge, just somewhere in between the two. I can take the couch tonight if that's easier."

"I'm not putting you out on my couch. Nobody sleeps on my couch. This is your bed. You will sleep in it. I'm little, I don't take up a lot of space. It's my personality that's big."

And her mouth, I think to myself while biting my tongue to keep from verbalizing the thought. "Alrighty

65

then, here's your pill. There should be a bottle of water in the mini fridge, just grab one and let's get some sleep."

I sit down on my side of the bed as Angelica takes her pill for the night and climbs into bed. Getting comfortable, I hear her say goodnight and it isn't long before her breathing changes and she's asleep. Reaching up, I turn off my lap and get comfortable on my side.

13

ANGELICA

WARM AND COZY. I let out a gentle moan as I roll my neck and find I'm locked in. I can't move. There are arms wrapped securely around me. What's more is the hands connected to those arms. Yeah, well, they are up my shirt just inches from my tits! If his thumb twitches, he'll be full on grabbing my boob. He's also pressed right up against me, his knee between my legs and his cock pressed against my ass. I'd be appalled if I wasn't waking from a dream where he'd just ravished me six ways from Sunday and twice on Thursday. I try and wiggle my way out of it and his grip tightens as his knee lifts. Not good. I reach behind me, giving him a gentle push on the stomach, but it doesn't work. He mutters something in his sleep that I don't understand.

"Maverick?" I whisper. Nothing. I take his hands and pull them up to my tits. Maybe a handful of that will bring him to life. "Maverick?"

He finally groans a little, his leg sliding down and taking the majority of his weight off me, letting me turn in his flexing arms. I wrap my fingers into his T-shirt and pull him in for a morning kiss.

"You broke your line, mister." I smile.

"No, you broke yours," he says, looking around as I lift his shirt and kiss his chest. I find more ink. The twisted tree continues across his pectoral. I lick down to his ribs and find a verse that looks like scripture. *'I can do all things through Christ who Strengthens me.'*

"Hmm, I don't know… I didn't move and found you wrapped around me." I smile, my tongue ring tracing the lines of his abs. I'm faced with the internal dilemma; do I leave his boxer briefs on him and keep torturing us both or do I risk him tossing me off and go for it? I push him down so he's on his back and his shirt is still up half way as I sit on top of him.

"What are you doing?" He watches me, though he doesn't touch me.

"Taking advantage of my kissing privileges and your sleepy disposition." I pull off my top and crush myself against him. My very hard nipples rub his heated flesh as my mouth seeks to find his once again. His hands find my hips and pull me forward and back. I can feel his cock as it dances under me. Oh God, I want that, but I promised him no sex. I know he's gonna flip if we do much more, but he's also gonna be hurting if I leave him like this. Hell, I'm gonna be hurting if I leave it like this.

I break the kiss and drag my body down him, grabbing his underwear, pulling at them. He hesitates.

"I just need to get it in my mouth… I promise." I smile convincingly, toying at the waistband. He stares at me, his chest rising and falling more quickly as he runs a hand down his face, a sure sign he's about to give in.

He licks his lips and nods yes. I pull as he lifts his ass and I've got him out of the confines of his boxer briefs. My lips curl up into a pleased grin as I take in the view. His cock is big, thick and long, a little curved, but nothing too drastic. The vein underneath is pulsing, he's so fucking hard. I start out stroking him with my hands and can't help but notice another tattoo, a huge dream catcher starting on his hip and ending just about his knee. Tangled in the webbing are jewels and a compass pointing due North. It's quite beautiful. I use my legs to part his and am nestled between them as he watches me. I take to his cock and his head hits the pillow. It may have been a couple of years since I've had one in my mouth, but it's like riding a bike, you never forget.

I'm right in the middle of my deep throat when I feel him tense up. Seriously?

"Angelica..." he tries to warn me, but I feel it, so I know. I pull back and he starts to come. I suck him till he stops twitching, swallowing down every salty drop before lifting my head again.

I look at the clock and see that it's eight-fifteen. Doc Peters will be here at ten. I grab my T-shirt and sit up. "I need to get moving. See you at breakfast in twenty?" I ask, kissing his cheek as I step over the cat on the floor.

✻ ✻ ✻

I'm not sure if leaving him like that was the smuttiest or the smoothest thing I've ever done. It was certainly the most guy-like thing I've ever done, seeing as I came like a rushing river too. I hop in the shower and get dressed for the day. It's Monday, so after Doc Peters, I have some work to do in the attic and then my room, provided the washer is here by then. It should be here by noon. Maverick said something about my garden, don't know what that was about, but I guess we'll see.

I wander out to the kitchen to help with breakfast and Maverick is standing there whisking some eggs like they up and killed his momma.

"Hey." I touch his forearm and he damn near jumps. "Easy." I chuckle, taking the eggs from him. "You should be more relaxed than this," I say, backing him up to the counter. "Do you know that you made me come too?" I whisper, gripping his shirt.

"I didn't do anything," he answers me.

"You getting off was like a chain reaction, it sent me right into overdrive." I search his eyes, I don't know if he's looking for an escape route or a place to pin me. Realizing he's conflicted, I pull away and switch gears. "What's on the menu?"

He looks to the silver bowl. "Eggs?"

I laugh. Okay, I seem to have broken him. I go to the fridge and grab fresh peppers, onions, and low-fat cheese, along with some potatoes and ham. "Western omelets and home fries with whole wheat toast? Maybe a fruit cup too?"

"If that's what you want."

"What I want isn't on the menu." I softly chuckle, turning from him and grabbing a knife to cut the veggies. I look over my shoulder and he's collapsed against the counter, his head in his hands. Yup, I done gone and broke my new manny.

✤ ✤ ✤

No sooner had we finished eating than the gate buzzes, and Doc Peters arrives, the car service having brought her a whole twenty minutes early. I answer the door and turn to introduce her to Maverick, but he

70

seems to have disappeared.

"Hello, Angelica." She smiles, looking around as I lead her into the living room so we can be comfortable. "You have a lovely home."

"Thank you, and thank you for being willing to come out here."

"I have to say, I was surprised to get your call. I had been made to understand, by one Maverick Donovan, that he was going to be tending to your therapeutic and medication needs for at least the next ninety days."

"Well…" I say as she sits. "See, I- We are in confidence, yes?"

"Of course, Angelica. Always."

"See, Maverick and I have sorta fallen into it."

She adjusts her sitting position uncomfortably. "Angelica, that's not good. He's in a position of authority over you. It's a gross misuse of his position."

"No, see, it happened before he started his therapy. All he'd managed to make me do was yell and scream a bit and well, come…"

"Angelica, I don't know that this is a good thing for you."

"I think this is exactly what I need. Someone like you to take care of my mind while someone like him helps me take care of my body and my soul. We've set boundaries, like no sex. We're going to take time to get to know each other. I've never done that. I'm usually the fuck um' and go type. So, this is new for me. In the meantime, he's going to help keep me on the straight and narrow and help keep me sober. How can that be wrong?"

Doc Peters shakes her head. "Angelica, you've been used and misused in your past. Are you sure he's not taking advantage of you? You have rights if you feel like he is."

"No, if anything, I'm taking advantage of him. I'm the one that's winning over here. I get all the benefits, and all he gets is a broken, sad excuse for a rockstar. I mean, look at me, I'm skinny and look like I've been through the ringer a few times. Lord knows I've been around the block more than once. I'm a slut, skank, whatever they wanna label me as, I pretty much have been. I'm virtually washed up and I'm only twenty-three. I've got seven implanted teeth because the drugs destroyed mine, plus the three from Brent's wife knockin' them out. I'm a fuckin' mess." The tears start to fall as my Louisiana drawl comes to the surface. "Da fact dat he wants me a'tall is amazin' to me."

"Have you told him about your past? About the abuse, the rapes, the baby?" she presses.

"Not yet, but we'll get there. It's early yet." I sob. "I don't wanna fuck this up by droppin' dat bomb on him too."

Doc Peters nods. "Just know that this is unorthodox. Typically, we say that you should wait to start a relationship after rehab, but since you've never really had a relationship, perhaps you will benefit from one. Your issue is that you isolate and have no close personal ties, including your band mates. Maybe he can help change that for you."

"I hope so." I sniff.

❊ ❊ ❊

Eleven o'clock comes fast and Doc Peters leaves. She'll be back at eight a.m. Wednesday, and then again Friday at eight a.m. I explained that earlier would be better as I have things around the house that take up much of the day and it would be best to not interrupt them. She agreed and set her schedule accordingly. I like her. More importantly, I trust her. She works for me and not the label.

I set myself to go help with lunch, but find Maverick isn't in the kitchen. I check outside, figuring maybe he's reading on the patio, nope. I knock on his door. There's no answer, but when I check the knob, it's unlocked. I open the door and find him sitting on the bed with his head in his hands. He looks completely stressed out and I don't know why.

"Maverick, what's wrong?" I ask, going up to him and standing right in front of him.

"You told her," he says, panicked.

"Told her? You mean Doc Peters? About you and me? Yeah, why wouldn't I?"

He sighs hard. "I- I won't be able to stay now." He sounds sad as he stares at the floor.

"What? Why?"

"Because it's not right. You heard what she said." He looks up at me, distraught.

"Wait, how do you even know what we were saying?" I ask, stepping back.

"I walked passed. You were in the living room."

"Well, did you stay for the whole talk or just her accusation part?"

"I heard what she had to say. I was done, I didn't need to stay for anymore."

"Well, if you had, you would have heard me tell her how good you have been for me so far. How I don't think about drugs around you. How we have set up boundaries, how you wanna get to know each other first. That I want to try harder because of you. All things she thinks are positives. She thinks you are a positive," I finish, cupping his face in my hands. "And I do too."

"What happens if she tells somebody?"

"I have her ass. It was during a session, so she can't. She's bound by confidentiality, so I'd have her license. You and me, we're not doing anything ethically wrong, she confirmed that for me."

He runs his hand down his face, and then across his thighs as I step in between them. "We're gonna be A-Okay," I say, running my fingers through his hair. He's so tense. I can feel it radiating off him. "Come here. Lay on your stomach and take off your shirt."

"Why?"

"Because you, my dear man, need to have those tense muscles worked over and I just so happen to have taken classes in massage therapy."

"I don't think that's a good idea," he says as I slip behind him on the bed and begin to pull up his shirt. Christ, more ink! He's got full angel wings on his back!

I trace the wings with my fingers and push him forward a tad. "You need this, now lay down."

"I'm pretty sure you're no angel," he groans, laying down finally.

"Oh, but I am. It's just that my wings are black," I whisper, licking up his spine.

14

MAVERICK

TODAY MARKS TWO WEEKS AND WHILE Angelica spent her Thursday doing her regular morning routine, I talked with Christy about our progress. He wasn't exactly happy that I agreed to a different counselor without talking to him, but it happened. I let him know that she's not afraid of work, yet at the same time, the girl can't sit still to save her life. I also mentioned incorporating her bandmates, one at a time, after the first thirty days. He agreed it'd be a good thing for her and that he'd talk to them.

As for myself, the last two weeks have been pure hell. I've thought more times than not about what it'd be like to touch Angelica in all the ways I know I can't. She's picked basketball for today and I'm already dreading it. She knows good and well that all she has to do is wiggle her ass against my cock and I need to stop. One of these days, the girl is going to push too far and she's going to get exactly what she deserves.

I head into the kitchen where Angelica should be working on lunch. Now that it's been two weeks, she also begins cooking most meals. I will usually keep doing breakfast, but leave her with lunch and dinner. By the ninety-day mark, she will be doing all meals on her own as well as meal prep. Day ninety is going to be a sad day for me. At the rate she's going, she isn't going to need me.

"What's with the sad puppy dog eyes?" Angelica asks, stirring me from my thoughts.

"Just thinking."

"About?" Eyebrows knitted together, she looks at me concerned.

"How well you are doing." I smile at her.

Angelica stops what she's doing, walking over to me. "And that's cause for a sad face? Geez, I'm sorry I'm so thorough."

"Yes," I laugh, "you won't need me after the ninety days at this rate."

Angelica stretches up on her tiptoes and pecks me on the lips. "But I'll probably want you, so no sad face."

I put a palm on each cheek. "You don't understand. If you don't need me, I have to find work elsewhere."

"Well, I'll keep you on as a personal trainer and everything else you may be doing here."

"Cupcake, if this ever moves passed what it is now, I can't work for you." I bring my lips to ghost across hers. "I've got to battle with myself to make it thirty days and you are so much stronger than you would ever believe you are."

Angelica swallows and looks down. "If you weren't here, I'd be strung out somewhere."

"Yes, at the beginning, you would have been. You are so different from day one," I say, pulling her face to look up into my eyes.

She shies away. "Every night, I've lain in bed and

I've thought about hopping in the car and going down to the strip, except when I was in yours."

"Why haven't you told me this?"

"Because if I climb back in that bed, we're not going to stop like we did last time and I won't put you in that position. So, I'm working it through, busting my butt around here and taking my medication."

"If I had known you needed to be in there, I would have figured it out. You should know that by now."

Angelica smiles. "It's okay, problem-solving is part of it. Isn't it?"

"Yes, but it's for later. Maybe you aren't ready for me to start bringing your bandmates in. Fuck. This is why I don't like someone else doing the counseling. I don't know what's going on."

"If you wanna know what's going on, then ask me. We need to learn to communicate like regular people. I don't know how to do that."

"When have I ever talked to you like a regular person? I think and talk like a counselor."

Angelica smiles. "You're doing pretty good right now."

"That's only because I'm eating a hole through my cheek. I want to go into my natural way so bad it's killing me. It's probably neck and neck with you and your shower head." I smirk at her.

Angelica presses up against me. "If you're hearing me, that's not the shower head." She runs her fingers down my cheek and across my lips and nips at them with a brow raised in question.

Angelica wraps her arms around my neck. "Ask and ye shall receive."

"What am I asking?"

She smirks at me. "I don't know, you tell me. What

do you want?"

"What are you making for lunch?"

Angelica's hands slide down from my shoulders to my chest. As she pats me, her head drops in defeat. "Blackened Cajun catfish, a side of spicy Cajun rice with butter lettuce and herb salad to start."

"Sounds good."

"Don't know what I'm doing for dinner, but there's a peach cobbler in the slow cooker for dessert. We can have it with some frozen yogurt."

"You're really enjoying being able to cook what you want, huh?"

"It's not about cooking what I want, it's about cooking what I know. And I know Cajun."

"So, if this isn't what you want, then tell me what it is and I can teach or we can learn together."

"Well, this is good, but what I want is a Po'boy."

"Within reason, Angelica."

"Muffuletta?"

"Do I even need to answer that?"

"Can I earn them? Like, earn cheat days? Or maybe exercise extra for calorie intake?"

"You're on a specific diet for a reason. It's to help maintain your health and well-being."

"So, I can't have good food again? No comfort foods?"

"No bad for you foods."

"So, that's a no."

"Yes, that's a no."

Angelica walks back over to the stove. She looks like someone stole her puppy. At this point, I can't make her happy. I excuse myself to check the mail. Just as I head out the door, Frank, one of the new guards for the front comes strolling up the walk with a package in his hands.

"Someone's got something special," Frank says.

I shake my head with a smile, taking everything from him. "Thanks, Frank."

"Any time, Maverick." He waves and is headed back down the walk.

I take the mail back to my room and set it on my bed to look it over. The box is for Angelica and looks to be from her daughter, but all the same, I still need to check it. Once I get the box open, I pull out two bears, one dressed as Belle and the other as Beast which makes me chuckle but is so suiting. There's a card, pictures, and looks to be a letter.

I get everything wrapped back up and set it in my closet so I can give it to Angelica tomorrow when I make Po'boys for her. I head back out to the kitchen to see if lunch is ready.

15

ANGELICA

IT'S FIVE A.M. AND *MY BIRTHDAY.* Today, I am twenty-four years old and it's the first time in ten years that I'm not already stoned out of my mind. This time last year, I was sleeping it off in a Sacramento holding tank after a binge, my hair all disheveled and coke still on the edges of my nose. The only thing that kept me from getting locked up was the killer blow job I'd given the arresting officer. Thinking back, most of my birthdays have sucked. I don't expect this one to be much different. See, the last time I was sober for a birthday was the night I got pregnant. I get up and shower, getting dressed for the day. I put on jeans and my boots with a blue tank top and matching sports bra. It's a blue kinda day. Since I know Maverick is asleep, I decide to go down to the stable and see Mason, my Palomino stallion. Maybe the ride will do me some good before breakfast.

I get to the stable and he's restless. I stroke his muzzle and he whinnies. I get the latch up and go inside to groom him and give him oats before saddling him up.

My handler, Lori, is off today, so I'll have to feed and water him, but that's okay, I don't mind it. The two Harlequin mares, Sadie and Gretchen, need running too, but I adore Mason. He's got more spirit and today, I need that thunder between my legs. I get him saddled and take him out onto the property. It's only five-thirty and the Nevada sun is already shaping it up to be a hot one. I push Mason into a run and the wind whipping against my skin feels good, like strong hands caressing me. My mind clears when I'm out here like this and that's just what I need.

✵ ✵ ✵

I'm back in the house by six-thirty and I find my pill is on the counter with a glass of water, my breakfast right next to it. Guess he's leaving me to my own devices today. It's Friday, so I've got the living room, sauna, and the grill to clean, but I can skip the grill since I cleaned it after we used it the other night. I also got the Doc coming at eight. I eat quickly, do my dishes, and then go toss on my tennis shoes and get to the living room, so I can at least have that done by the time Doc Peters comes.

Sure enough, the car brings her early by about twenty minutes, as usual. I answer the door and she is all smiles to my half-frown.

"Well, happy birthday!" she exclaims, coming inside.

"I suppose," I mutter as we head for the living room.

"You not celebrating it in any fashion? A special meal, a cake of some sort?" she asks, concerned. "You should do something. It's important, it's a milestone."

"Eh, I'm sober, that's enough. I think I'm just going

to go along with my day. Better that way, not to make a fuss. Besides, who's here to really celebrate with? Maverick and I are still on the fence with things and what I'd like to do... Well... He's still not... He says we're not ready."

"And he's right, Angelica. You need to slow down, take your time here."

"I know," I groan. "But at this rate, I'm going to explode! The man walks into the room and all I want to do is put his cock in my mouth."

Doc Peters laughs. "Well, I guess that's better than a line up your nose, but you need to stop looking at him as your new drug. You need to look at him as an opportunity, a shot at something good, and good *for* you but separate *from* you."

I nod. "I think I understand. I need to take stock of me and realizes he's not my savior."

"Yes. Precisely. He's also not just a tool of your sobriety, he is a person with feelings and a life that will continue beyond you."

I sit back and take in what she is saying. He was saying something similar, yesterday at lunchtime, about him having to move on. I don't want him to do that. I can make him very comfortable here with me if he would just open up to me and let me take care of him a bit. Christ, how is it that I've gone from the crazy bitch to snuggle bunny in just a few weeks? Is this the sober me? Is this woman even capable of being a rockstar? I wonder, and that wondering has me scared shitless. Christ, I want a drink or something to stop these racing thoughts.

I'm pacing now. I've finished with my chores, there's still time till lunch, and I haven't seen Maverick all damn day. It would figure the one fucking day when

I feel like I really need him, he would up and disappear on me.

I'm twitchy and can't seem to calm myself down. The deep breathing exercises aren't helping and sitting makes my legs shake even harder. I can't stop the tears that keep flowing either as I collapse on my bedroom floor, a mess of emotions.

My phone goes off at ten to twelve, the alarm sounding to me that I need to move my ass back to the kitchen. I know I can't let him find me like this, he'll never believe I'm not high. I yank myself off the floor, wipe at my tear stained face, and go to the bathroom. There's nothing I can do about the puffiness of my eyes at this point. I just splash water on my face and head back out of the room to see what I'm not ready to eat.

The kitchen is filled with a familiar smell. There's spices and I swear something is being deep fried. My stomach jumps excitedly as I spot Maverick. He has his back to me, fussing with something. I stand there hugging myself, unsure if I want to speak. I look at the counter and see a box that looks as if it has little hearts and angel wings drawn on it as well as two of the totes filled with my stuff from his room. I swallow, seems he's been busy while I've been freaking out and silently cursing him.

I go over to the box and realizing it's from my little girl, I tear into it. I find two adorable little bears dressed as the lead characters from *Beauty and the Beast*. They're from one of those *Build-A-Bear* places, so that means that Alec, Janice, and she took a day out to take the time to make them. The last time I saw her, we watched the animated version. Seems she remembered. I bite my lip as I look at the pictures of my flaxen haired little princess and have to be careful as I cry, not to get them wet with my tears.

I look up and see Maverick has turned to me and is watching me closely.

"She just turned nine in April. I'm sure my accountant sent something nice because I was in rehab, but nothing like this, not so thoughtful or genuine." I sniffle. "God, I miss her so much," I moan.

"You know, once you're better, you can always get her back."

"I wouldn't know what to do with her. How am I supposed to take care of her and go on tour, and do shows, and junkets, and press? I can't be a mommy and a Rockstar."

"You'd figure it out, that's the point." He stays where he is, not moving, ever the rock. What I wouldn't give for some emotion out of him, something other than non-judgmental understanding. I know there's a passionate man under there, *a compassionate man*, I just need to find him. I wish he'd hold me, touch me kindly, something, but I know I'm not going to get that. Not now. I have to find a way to break through his shell, to show him he's broken through mine.

"I just wanna see her. It's been more than two years since I've seen her. That was the last time I was sober enough and we were touring the area. I snuck away for two days to just be with her. The label went nuts looking for me." I laugh shortly. "I didn't care. We were too close for me not to run to her." I turn the picture to him. "I'm just glad she looks like me and not *him*."

"She's just as beautiful as her momma," he says softly.

I smile, picking up the card, typical I love you, Momma. Then there is a hand-written letter. Her penmanship is all over the place, but it's adorable just the same.

Mommy, I love you. I miss you. Alec and Janice are good to me. We are coming to Nevada. Maybe if you are there, we can see you.

Then the handwriting changes and it's Janice. She explains that Alec needs to see a specialist in the area and they hope that while they are awaiting the test results, that perhaps, Angela can see me. It's been a long time and she asks about me more and more. She finishes by explaining that it is important that we see each other and that I need to call her soon. She leaves their number and her regards.

I clear my throat and look up at Maverick, fear beginning to cling to me. Something isn't right, I can feel it in my bones.

"What's wrong?"

"I- They're coming to Nevada." I drop the letter into the box and close it all up.

"When?"

"The first week of July, apparently, something is going on with Alec, her foster father. He's having to see a specialist, having tests run. Janice says it's important that I see them," I grit out, going back into the box and fishing out the letter, sliding it across the table to him in case he thinks I'm lying. I'm back on edge, feeling like the room is closing in on me.

He opens the letter, scanning it before looking back at me. I'm standing here bouncing on the balls of my feet, my jaw clenched so tightly that my teeth hurt something fierce.

"Why don't you call?" he asks straightly.

"You have my phone," I whisper. "I don't have the number memorized. I mean, who does nowadays?" I mutter.

"You could have asked for it for that reason. I'm not that big of a dick." He puts the letter down.

"I figured it would be me askin' for a favor. Didn't wanna be doin' that."

He clears his throat and sighs with a shake of his head. "It's different, you have a daughter, you can call her if you want. I just assumed you didn't call because from what you said, it didn't seem like you talked to her a whole bunch."

"I don't, not really. The occasional phone call every so often. A Skype call when I found myself lucid enough. I've been a terrible mother..." I trail off, my hands over my face. "I've seen her maybe two dozen times in nine years. I just... I was fourteen when she was born and they took her. What was I supposed to do? Then I was all alone, how was I gonna take care of her? Being in the band takes all my time. This..." I hold out my hands. "This is the first time I've stayed in my own house for more than a few days since I bought the damn place!" I'm close to shouting now. "I have all this space and it's just wasted on me. All these rooms that I never use. I am always at a party or a club, always moving. It's better than the alternative. I should have sold the place a long time ago. Just stayed in hotels, like the trash I am. Kyle's got it right, he just holes up in the penthouses on the strip. Fuck all, why put down roots if there's no one to be rooted to?"

I fall to the floor, not caring what he thinks. I'm shattering, the idea of seeing her, knowing I have nothing to offer, breaks me.

16

MAVERICK

ANGELICA FALLS TO THE GROUND, bawling, and it damn near kills me. Standing back these past two weeks, letting her do everything on her own like I'm supposed to be doing is proving to be the death of me. No matter how much I battle with myself, I'm around the counter and on the floor, pulling her into my arms, running a hand through her hair. "Shh, calm down now. We have the rest of the month to get you ready to see her. I promise I won't let you fall." Angelica clings to me and sobs harder. "Hey now, dry those tears. I did not make this birthday lunch for you to cry through it."

"I'm sorry. I'm so sorry," she says through her sobs, her body shaking.

"You have nothing to be sorry for, but I'm going to tell you what, we're going to get off this floor, eat lunch, then you can pick whatever movie you want and we will cuddle on the couch for your birthday. How's that sound?"

Angelica sniffles and nods into my chest. "I'm sorry I'm such a mess. I don't know how to do this."

I turn Angelica so she's straddling me, so I can see her face. I lift my shirt, wiping her snot covered face with it before lifting her chin to make her look at me. "Cupcake, I've told you, I don't know how to do this thing we're doing any better than you know how to be sober."

Angelica looks down at my shirt then back to me. "That was a total *Manny* move and it is disgusting. Please take that off." I pull off my shirt. "Better. I guess we're both a couple of messes, but it's good to know you're not made of stone."

"I suppose so. I was only doing what I was supposed to be doing. I told you it wouldn't be easy and I promise it hasn't been easy."

Angelica wraps her arms around my neck. "Can you promise me something?" She searches my eyes.

"I can try."

She nods with a sheepish smile. "*Promise* me that you'll *try* to talk to me more. In any capacity."

"Me talking isn't what you need, though. Speaking of talking... How was your talk with the doc?"

"We talked about you," she answers, hanging off me almost playfully.

I just drop my head and wait to see if she says anything else.

"We talked about me needing to not see you as a crutch." I raise my head to look at her with my brow raised. "And my taking a more *proactive* approach to my sobriety."

"I think I might like this doc after all."

Angelica smiles at me. "We talked about my birthday and the stress that it causes me. Some of which, you just kind of witnessed. How it's the first one I've been sober for in nine years."

My counselor mind wants to ask about a million questions, but my heart just wants to pull her close, hold her to me, and not let anyone else hurt her. The question is… How in the hell do I explain all of this to Angelica? I look into Angelica's eyes so that I can gage her reaction. "What are we doing?"

"Currently, I'm throwing a tantrum and your staring at me."

"No. I mean this thing between you and me. What is it?"

"You want like a definition?" Angelica asks, getting out of my lap and standing off to the side.

"I would say clarification, but definition works just as well," I respond, standing as well.

Angelica is watching me, chewing on her thumbnail. "Well, I would say that we're dating, but you'd actually have to take me somewhere for that."

"You have another forty days, at least, before you can leave the house, so that's out. *Next.*"

"I don't know what you would call this. I mean I like you a lot. I'm attracted to you. I hope that the feeling is mutual."

This woman seriously doesn't help me out at all. I turn toward the counter behind me and smack my head on it. Next thing I know, I feel Angelica's hands on my shoulders and hear her laughing.

"You know, you make absolutely no sense and yet I still love listenin' to you talk. Of course, it's not what I was hopin' you were goin' to say." I turn to face her. "I know we haven't known one another long and I know we have a lot to learn about each other, but damn it, I want to try this thing. I want to know the nooks and crannies of you. I want you to feel comfortable around me. I want to be able to help you get ready to, hopefully, bring your daughter to live here with you. Angelica Emily Fontaine, I'm pretty sure you pushed through and made me fall in love with you. So, I need to know what we are doing here."

Angelica is looking at me like she's about to hyperventilate and all the while, she's chewing on her thumb. I'm not sure if I'm going to get hit, kissed, or what at this point.

"How?" Angelica asks. "How can you be in love with me? You barely know me and what you do know is so fucked up. I love hearing it, but don't say it just to say it." And she's crying again.

"How many women do you think I've said that to? Answer me that, first."

"I couldn't say," she barely whispers.

"You've spent a bit of time with me. I'm not an irrational person, nor am I someone that doesn't think everything out. So, think about it. How many?"

"Once, maybe twice."

"Never."

"Never?"

I step toward Angelica. "I've never felt for any girlfriend, a shred of what I've felt for you in two weeks."

Angelica drops her head to look at the floor and she's trembling, so I stop walking. "I'm afraid. I know what I feel and it's like being kicked by a mule. It's raw, its passionate, and I can feel you before you even enter the room. That scares me because it's out of my control. I'm afraid of what you'll do to my heart if I give it to you." Angelica looks up at me. "But, just the same, I want to. You've spent all this time taking care of me and I keep thinking of ways that I want to take care of you."

"I sit up most nights thinking about what happens

if we do this and then you go back on tour. You decide to hook up with someone. I'm not the kind of guy that can abide cheating. I don't care if it's male or female. You could break my heart tomorrow, Angelica, and there's not a damn thing I could do about it. You could tell me to leave today and I'd have to go. There are millions of possibilities, but none of them tell me what we are doing."

"Here's the problem… We're in limbo. We're not lovers, but we're more than friends. That needs to be corrected, but not today. We need to move forward. A kiss here and a kiss there does not a relationship make. At least, not with me. To be completely frank, you can't walk into a room without me wanting to jump on you, typically. So, we just need to get over the last hurdle, then we will have some form of definition."

"Can I come the rest of the way to you now, without the chance of getting hit?" I ask. Angelica looks at me, smiles, and nods. With two giant steps, I scoop her into my arms, wrapping her legs around my waist and arms around my neck. "I'd love to finish this conversation, but I'm pretty sure I made something you've been craving for lunch. So how about we go check it out?"

Angelica smiles and nods her head. "I'm starving."

17

ANGELICA

HE MADE ME SHRIMP PO'BOYS AND SWEET potato fries. I swear he even baked the baguette the sandwich is stacked on. Everything is fried in coconut oil or baked to cut the fat and keep the calories down. Genius. It is just the touch of Louisiana I've been craving.

"I have very few memories of home that I cling to," I say as I chomp down on a fry, catching Maverick's attention. "But the food stays with me. Cooking was something Mom and I did together before she married *him*." I half laugh. "I remember my tenth birthday, we baked this colossal honey cake. It's a cake filled with pecans and fruit, and butter and honey. It's just to die for and super simple to make. Anyway, I accidentally grabbed the self-rising flour instead of the cake flour and you can imagine what happened to the cake in the oven."

"Something like the washing machine, I imagine," Maverick says with a laugh.

"You know it." I laugh. "There was cake and batter

everywhere!" I throw out my hands. "But you know what my mom did? She just laughed and we cleaned it up. Then we sat there and ate the cooked parts right out of the pan with some vanilla ice cream. My mom was good like that, back then." I swallow hard, thinking about Stanley, my step-father. "Stanley changed all that. He murdered the laughter in our house and replaced it with dissonance, anger, and lies." I sit back in my chair and Maverick is watching me. I can see the questions in his eyes. The ones he wants to ask but doesn't dare.

"You said you wanted me to be comfortable with you. I want you to be the same way with me, but I'm afraid if I tell you certain things, you will become quite uncomfortable. I'm afraid I will drive you away before I even have you completely. Yet, not telling you the truth of things, not telling you my truth, is unfair to you. So, I'm going to tell you why today is such a burden on me, and then you can decide if everything you said earlier still rings so true. Okay?"

Maverick furrows his brow as I get up, putting out my hand to him. "You don't have to."

I insist with my open hand. "Yeah, I do." I walk him to the living room and sit him down in the big comfy chair and then I sit opposite him. I let out a long sigh, folding and unfolding my hands a few times before bringing my legs up under me.

"My real dad split before I was born. He was a jazz player and the music called him harder than the responsibility of being a father. It was okay though, my mom, she managed, waited tables in the local diner days and sang in a lounge three nights a week. She got my grandmother to watch me when I was too little to cart around. Then, when I was about three, she just brought me to work with her and stuck me in a chair with crayons and papers to play. Got easier when I started school, but the nights she worked, I still went with her, listening to her sing. I guess it's where I caught the bug and she encouraged me always. I did competitions. Won some, lost more. My voice was too rough for them, I suppose. Southern rock wasn't really a thing for little girls, ya know? Then, when I was twelve, she met Stanley at the diner. He was a mechanic and had just moved into town, starting his own garage and towing company. As big as Baton Rouge was, he was bound to make money. He and mom hit it off. I mean she was only thirty and looking good, and he was nice… At first. It wasn't all at once, they dated for over a year before they got married and I liked him just fine. He bought me pretty things, took me to my rehearsals, paid for my vocal classes, seemed like a real nice guy.

When he moved in, it all changed. He took off my bedroom door because he said he couldn't trust me because I had gotten a C in French, my first semester taking it. Claiming that I wasn't studying hard enough, he'd come into my room and stand over me, dictating it to me since he was Cajun through and through and like my mother, spoke it well. I just never had the tongue for it. I understand, but don't speak it well. Then his leering turned to rubbing my shoulders late in the night. He often barged in on me in the shower or the bath, saying he needed something from the medicine cabinet and then he would linger. I didn't know what to do. I tried saying something to my mom, but she said I was crazy. That he was my step-father and I was trying to make her mad at him because he was being mean to me. Then the drinking started. It was just a beer here and there at first. By then, he'd begun to hover near my room at night after mom went to bed." I look up, and Maverick is watching me, his expression soft, but unyielding as to his feelings. I'm sure he knows where this story is going, but I need to get it out of me.

"My fourteenth birthday, I had a party and there was a boy that I liked, Leonard Gaudet. He was like five-ten, fifteen, black hair, and dark chocolate eyes and skin. I thought I was in love. We had been flirting all year and I was so happy that he came to my party. I wore this lovely little white summer dress with a little black belt at the waist and black buckle shoes, my hair in curls. I was picture perfect that day. Mom had to work second shift, so she left half way through, but she got to see me all dolled up. Anyway, as the party progressed, so did Stanley's drinking. Eventually, the kids filtered out, parents coming to get them or on their own, as preteens do. Not Leonard though, he said he had a present for me other than the Britney Spears album he bought me. He took me up to my room and sat me on my bed and that's where he kissed me. My first real kiss. I was elated. That was until I was torn away from him by hard, ungentle hands and a roaring voice. Poor Leonard was so scared that he ran off as Stanley swore and threatened him.

Then Stanley turned his attention to me, calling me a little slut and a tease. I tried to get up, but he blocked me from moving as he pulled off his belt. I thought he was going to beat me with it. He told me to lift my dress and I sobbed, begging him not to hit me. He just laughed at me. I could smell the liquor on his breath as he leaned over me, his hand sliding between my tiny thighs. He told me that I'd been teasing him for months, but was going to give it up right then and there. He tore off my panties and forced himself into me, all the while threatening to kill me if I told, threatening to kill my mom if I told. Mom wound up having to work over that night, so he made use of me several more times. By the time morning came, I couldn't sit straight."

"I started acting out, stopped taking care of myself, hoping it would deter him, but when mom worked overnights, he'd get me in a shower and rape me all over again. After about a month, I found out I was pregnant with Angela. Terrified of what would happen if they found out it was his, I refused to say who the father was. They kept asking, but I've never said. That fuck knows she's his, but he'd never step up for her. I tried years ago to tell my mother what happened, tell her so she could get away from him, but she doesn't believe me. So I've cut ties. It's why I was emancipated. Having Angela was a smoking gun to the abuse. If Stanley hadn't talked my mom into allowing the emancipation, I would have come out with it and he'd have gone to prison. So, I took off on my own, but I was strung out and she was born addicted. She's okay now, has some minor learning impairments, but is otherwise a happy, healthy nine-year-old. I couldn't take care of her, so I agreed to have her put in foster care, but never signed off on adoption. She's been with Alec and Janice Theriot since she was two. They take such good care of her. I couldn't ask for better people. I tried to get her a couple of times, but I just couldn't stay clean. I like the drugs. I like the feel of being numb, being high, the ability to get so much done. They gave me an excuse for my racing thoughts, my bad behavior, my sleeping around. It could all be attributed to the drugs. That night, when I OD'd... I wasn't trying to kill myself. Not exactly. I was overwhelmed by the world around me and was just trying to drown out the noise. I needed someone to see that there was more to me than the hellcat, the cunty bitch, that I needed help, but there was no one to care because I'd pushed them all away. They were all too busy chasing Brent and his addictions, too busy trying to fix what I'd help to break out of spite and jealousy because he found what I couldn't and was fighting for it. I was just looking for a taste of oblivion. Now that I'm sober and can see the forest through the trees, I know it was all an excuse, a poor man's remedy for the disease of my past. I want to upcharge and feel like I finally am." I stop and fidget, waiting to see what he is going to say or do. I don't cry anymore, I've had my fill of that. I'm more afraid of what may happen now that he knows how screwed up I am.

"Is your mother still alive?" he asks almost immediately.

I nod. "Yes, they still live in Baton Rouge, right in the house I grew up in."

"Then I think it's time you make a phone call," he states matter-of-factly.

I stare at him. "Wh-what would I- could I possibly have to say? The last time she and I spoke, she made it pretty clear she didn't want to hear what she called my lies."

"As soon as you told me you had a daughter and how old she was, I did the math. I knew you were raped. I had to wait for you to be ready to tell it. That's not something you pry out of somebody. What I didn't know was who done it. I had my suspicions, but those only go so far. If she doesn't believe you, Angela is coming here, we can do a DNA test. Till he pays for what he put you through, you won't be able to get passed it."

"Yeah, but wouldn't Stanley have to consent to that too?"

"How much have you told Doc Peters?"

"Some of this, not quite all of that."

"With another client, we had to prove she wasn't lying through DNA and the courts mandated it. In cases like yours, with bipolar, multiple personalities, that kind of situation, and you think you know who the father is and want the DNA test, and the doctor and counselor come together and decide that it can help you move past some of your symptoms, the judge will sign off on it."

"You are basically telling me that I can't just bury this anymore."

"No, you can't bury it, because if you keep burying it, it's gonna keep coming up."

I bite my lip and nod my head. Maverick is asking me to face *him*. After all these years, to finally look Stanley in the face and put him in his place. Would the test hurt her? Could I really do this? "It's been nine years; can they really do anything now?" I ask softly.

"He can still go to prison and be held for child support." He chuckles.

I shake my head. "I never thought about it... I just wanted to get away, get us both away. I just wish my mother would've done the same."

"Do you know where the bipolar falls? On your mom or your dad?"

"No."

"That could have a lot to do with it."

I scoot to the edge of the couch and look him over. He's in therapist, white knight, savior mode, but that doesn't tell me how he feels. I stand up and walk over to him, placing my hand against his chin and making him look up at me. "Knowing how fucked up I am, knowing how deep the wounds are and just how much work I have ahead of me, do you still want to make a go of it with me? Try and build a relationship with this mess of a woman before you?"

He looks around curiously. "What mess?" He grins as I wrap my arms around his head, hugging him to me.

"Thank you," I whisper softly. "Thank you."

"For?" he asks, keeping his hands to himself, much to my chagrin. I could really use the tenderness right now. I push him back and sit down on him, wrapping my arms around him tighter.

"Thank you for taking a chance on me."

18

MAVERICK

AFTER ANGELICA AND I FINISHED TALKING about everything on her birthday, we did just as I suggested, cuddled and watched a movie. This week, on the other hand, has been a complete downward spiral on my part. Tomorrow is by far, one of the worst days of my life, Father's Day and my birthday wrapped in one. Usually, I'd ask for time off, but in this case, I can't. I can't leave Angelica right now. She needs me and I promised I wouldn't. So, no matter how hard it may be for me to walk around here and act as normal as I possibly can, that's exactly what I've been doing. I'm sure she's figured out something's wrong, but has been polite enough to either not ask, or she just doesn't want to know yet. I'm fine with either because they both keep her from asking questions I'd rather never answer.

I've spent my day in bed since I made Angelica breakfast this morning. Hell, I never even got dressed today. I've got a five o'clock shadow and she's never seen me not baby smooth. It's getting close to dinner time. I haven't turned on the desktop, but I've kept an eye on Angelica all day and I know that right now, she should be just about done making her dinner.

I face the door when I hear a knock and see it being nudged open by Angelica carrying a tray with what looks to be soup and something else. "Are you decent? You alive? Still breathing?"

"Well, not particularly, but as you are already in here, would it make a difference?"

"Snappy," Angelica says, walking over to me with the tray. "Someone is in rare form."

"I'm sure everything you made tastes great, but I'm not really up for eating."

Angelica looks around before setting the tray so it's straddling my legs and puts her hand on my stomach. "You don't appear to have a fever, so you need to eat, seeing as I haven't seen you eat a damn stitch all week."

"I'm not hungry."

Angelica looks around again before letting her eyes settle back on me. "You're obviously not sick, so what's going on? This room smells like a bear's cave and you look like something they'd be rollin' around in."

I run a hand through my hair and down my face. "It's a rough weekend for me. One that I'd much rather forget," I say with a huff.

She sits gently on the bed beside me, furrowing her brow and looking at me. "What's going on?"

"Looks can be deceiving. This week is my hell and I've done good up till today."

"That doesn't tell me much."

"Did you know my birthday is nine days after yours?" Angelica shakes her head no. "Well, it is and this year, it also again lands on Father's Day."

She watches me, confused. "Tomorrow's Father's Day? It completely slipped my mind."

"Yeah, well, I really wish it could slip mine," I state matter of factly.

"No wonder you've been out of sorts."

"It's just a hard week. No sister, no father, and we never met our mother."

"You said you were twelve when your dad died."

"I was." I nod.

"So, what happened to you and your sister? Without a momma, who took care of you?"

"We were split up. She went to a girls' home and me a boys'. I was fifteen when I got the news that she'd followed suit with my father. I was watched like a hawk and only lasted two months before getting out my own."

"So, that's what you meant when you said you couldn't save her?"

"If they'd only kept us together, I could have kept her from succumbing to the depression."

"You mean like you are at the moment?" she asks with a raised brow.

"There's a big difference. I would never touch the drugs or alcohol. Yes, I spend a week remembering shit I'd much rather forget, but's it's just about always forefront in my mind."

"But you know as well as I do that laying here, stinking up the joint, isn't going to help. Do something to honor them instead of mourning them."

I rub a hand over my face and jerk a little. She's got me pinned, so I can't go anywhere. "How exactly do you expect me to throw a party for selfish people who only ever cared about themselves? Angelica, I did not grow up like you. We mourn, not throw parties," I snap.

Angelica straightens up a bit. "Maybe you don't throw a party, but the wallowing doesn't help. It doesn't help them. It doesn't help you. It doesn't help *anybody*.

You don't come out of it any better. All you end up with is an empty stomach, dirty sheets, and a lonely room." She stands. "But if that's what you want, *fine*. If not, I'll be at the stables."

"I don't mean to snap, *damn it*. Usually, I take this week and next week off, but I couldn't leave *you*." I move the tray away from my lap and look at her. "Am I not supposed to have bad days? Did I fuck up my job with you so bad that you actually think if I knew a better way for me to cope, I wouldn't be doing it? Trust me, I've studied it for years and nothing else has ever worked for me," I snarl to her back as she is walking out the door.

She stops, looking back at me. "I'm not sayin' you can't have a bad day or a bad week. But what you damn well need to do is fuckin' communicate it to me. You might be in a hole, but I'm not doin' so hot myself this week. You don't hear me bitchin' and moanin'. Now, I understand rough. I understand dark. I even understand wantin' to climb into a black hole, but damn it, this is my house. Give me a little respect. Last week, you tell me you love me and this week, you don't even talk to me. So, what the fuck do you think I'm supposed to be thinkin'?"

Respect. I'm going to fucking show her respect. I've done nothing but fucking respect her. I've not touched her and I've done everything I'm fucking supposed to be doing. "Who the hell do you think you are talking to? First, to talk about respecting you. You should have a fucking package with everything you would need for this week. I sat it in your room. I know what this week is for you, which is exactly why I didn't want you to have to deal with this." I take a deep breath. "Ya know what? Come with me," I order, walking passed her and to her room. Opening the door, I walk in and grab the box from beside the dresser and set on the bed. "There, go ahead and open it, and then tell me I don't respect you. No matter what you may think, I've done nothing but fucking respect you."

Angelica walks over and opens the box, then looks at me, shaking her head. She sighs. "Thank you for this, but if I had a choice between what's in the box and you normal, I'd rather have you. I mean, if we're going to do this and you're having a hard time, you need to share it with me, not block me out. That what's got me so upset."

"That's just it, I've been alone for twelve years. I've never once cared in all these years about being alone until now. At the same time, I worry about what it could do to you. So, don't ever, not even for one second, think that no matter what I'm doing, I didn't think about you first. I tried hard to be a normal person. More than I ever have in my life. For you, this week."

Angelica looks up at me. "I'd kiss you right now, but you have unbelievable dragon breath."

I shake my head. "I'm sure I do."

"You're impossible." She smiles.

I look down at myself before giving myself a pinch. "I'm pretty sure I'm possible. I even double checked and yup, the pinch still hurts."

Angelica walks over to me, giving me a push toward the door. "Go take a shower, eat, and then meet me at the stables and come for a ride with me."

"Um…" I pause. "Can I just wait till your back? I don't do horses."

Angelica gives me a funny look. "You're a country boy with no horse experience?"

"I didn't really have money to have horses around

when I was growing up and I sure didn't live in a neighborhood where we could keep one."

"I really wanted you to come riding with me," Angelica pouts.

"I can't ride one today. So, how about starting next week, when you go to the stables, unless you don't want me, I will come with. I need to get to know the horses before riding. I can't just get on one without knowing them first. Okay?" I plead with her.

Angelica smiles and nods. "Okay, I can live with that."

"Good. Now, go enjoy your ride. Just don't stay out too late, it's getting dark."

She looks to the ceiling. "I don't want to go riding by myself. You go take your shower. I'll have my supper and perhaps I'll spend the rest of the night straddling you on the couch."

"I think you need to work off some of your excess energy, but we can't go there. You know this."

"With my clothes *on*. I'm not destroying my furniture. *Sheesh*."

"Angelica, we can both only handle so much of you straddling me."

"Okay, so half the night." She smiles seductively.

I drop my head. "Cupcake, I don't have the control I need for you to straddle me at all at this point. Especially with you kissing and rocking against me."

Angelica gets up in my space, smirking. "I know, now go take your shower."

She pushes out the door and I'm left wondering what in the hell she has up her sleeves.

19

ANGELICA

I HAVE TO BE STEALTHY as I go to my library while he's in the shower to find the perfect gift for him. I've seen his collection of reading material. From classics to modern romances, Maverick reads it all. I go for one of my favorite books, *Alice's Adventures in Wonderland*. It's a leather bound, first edition. Took me a bit of time to find it, especially since it's signed by Carroll himself. It's worth a mint, but that's not why I have it. I simply love the story, and have several versions of it, regardless of its pseudo-political diatribe. I get lost in the fantasy of it. I think he will love it too. At least I hope he will.

I'm sitting on the couch when I hear him come padding out into the living room, finally. I've changed into my usual nightly attire, little pink silk shorts and a cami with matching silk button down cover. I have the shark week survival kit next to me and have leaned into the Hershey's kisses with a vengeance already. God, thank you for bringing me a man who understands the need to throw chocolate at a bleeding vagina. Add in the gallons of soda pop and Midol and he's perfect. I look back at him and he's showered and wearing crisp, dark indigo jeans and a nice, clean, dark gray T-shirt that fits him just right. I smile, holding up a KitKat to him, waving him over as I scroll through the On-Demand selection.

"Chocolate's all yours, I'm not eating it, thanks though." He waves me off, sitting down next to me. I pull up my legs, slapping them right down into his lap, the box on my tummy.

"Don't know if I can trust a man that doesn't eat chocolate," I tease. Seeing there is a Harry Potter Marathon on one of the higher channels, I ask, "This look good to you?"

"We can watch whatever you wanna watch."

"I'm just thinkin' background noise," I say, popping another chocolate. "You sure you don't want some?" I shake my foot in his lap slowly. He's positioned my feet so they don't hit his cock, but I know he's thinking a million different things.

"No, I'm good. I don't want any chocolate." He shakes his head, still looking straight at the television. Ugh, men. I wanna play a little and he's on full alert, as usual. God, I wish he wasn't wound so tight. I put down my box and scoot down the couch to him, pulling myself into his lap so I'm sitting like a little kid, an arm wrapped around his neck.

"Sorry I was bitchy today," I say, rubbing his chest in a slow circle.

"As opposed to any other day?" he drops.

"Seriously?" I give him a gentle shove as I straddle him. "So not fair!" I giggle. Getting in his face, my lips a breath from his, I say, "Just because I'm hard headed, doesn't mean-" I break into a sputtering of laughter. I can't finish the sentence. "I'm a bitch, I own it," I finish, dropping my head onto his shoulder. I notice his hands haven't left the couch, so I slide mine over his. Lacing my fingers into his, I pull his hands up onto my hips as my tongue darts out of my mouth, tracing his freshly shaven neck and jaw.

He clears his throat, lifting his head as I hover over him, my eyes searching his. His need to control his impulses astounds me. I wonder what he'd be like if he let go? Even for an instant, surrendered to his needs and let himself just be...

"*Kiss me*," I whisper ever so softly, my thighs tightening against his sides as my fingers dance up his tensing arms, his hands still sitting on my hips.

He lifts his face to mine, his lips connect softly but far too briefly before they are gone once more. I look down at him, my brow furrowed, my bottom lip between my teeth.

"So, we can't even kiss now?"

"We can't when it leads... When it could lead to other things."

"Don't you think I have at least some self-control? I mean, isn't that what all of this is about? Me gainin' control over me? I wanna make out with my boyfriend, is that so bad?" I sit back so I can see his face more easily.

He drops his head back on the couch, looks up at the ceiling, and murmurs, "Killing me."

I laugh a little. "What's that mean?" I strum my fingers on his abs, watching him closely.

"It means I'm going to Hell." He looks at me with a groan.

"At least you'll go with a smile on your face." I grab him by the chin and crush my mouth against his and this time, when I open my mouth to deepen the kiss, so

108

does he as his hands tighten around my back.

***

I wake up in my bed, all alone. I must have fallen asleep on the couch. Maverick and I spent the better part of the night kissing with me grinding on him like we were a couple of teenagers before finally settling down into watching *The Half-Blood Prince*. It's about four-thirty, so I get up, deciding that I'm going to make breakfast since it's his birthday.

I take out the yellow and red bell peppers we have and decide on a different take on the western omelet with ham. I whisk up all the other ingredients and pour them into the halved peppers to bake. I'll add a bit more cheese at the end with scallions for a finishing touch. That done, I mix up some cranberry orange muffins, start the hash browns and turkey sausage, and pull out oranges for fresh squeezed juice. I'm juicing the oranges when I hear the jingle of Lucille's bell, telling me that her master isn't far behind. I've come to an arrangement with the cat. I give her my food and she goes away. Today, she has her own little plate of meats and eggs. I'm putting the plate down when I hear Maverick clear his throat.

I turn with a smile. "Hey, good morning." I watch as he grabs Lucille and the plate.

"What do you think you're doing?" he asks, his voice on high alert.

"Um, feeding the scavenger like I always do."

"You feed her people food?"

"Yes, we have an arrangement."

"What makes you think that's okay?"

"It's just eggs and meat, no veggies like onions or

anything that can hurt her."

"She doesn't eat people food." He's getting angry with me.

"Um, tell her that because she's constantly begging off me."

"Then you smack her nose and send her away."

I suddenly feel sorry for the cat, we're in the same boat, can't have what we want even though it's right there in front of us.

"I'm sorry," I say. "I won't do it again."

"It's fine, I just wish you would've asked first. I pay good money for her food and she hasn't been eating it. At least now, I know why."

I chuckle softly, reaching out and scratching her head. "Seems we're both going back to our diets." I look to the stove and go to the sink, washing my hands before returning to it. "I've got the main dishes in the oven, should be done in like fifteen. I just finished the orange juice, help yourself and have a seat," I say, hoping he'll see the package wrapped neatly in aluminum foil with a bow on the counter.

"Looks like you've been more than busy," he observes, looking around curiously from behind me, which makes me smile. He's seen it now, I'm sure.

"Whatever do you mean?" I shake my ass a little as I turn the hash browns over.

"How did you get something for me?"

I pull the stuffed peppers from the oven and check the muffins, just a few more minutes, before turning to him. I smile. "Open it if you like."

He stares at it, then back at me a few times as though he doesn't know what to do.

"It's not poisoned or booby trapped." I walk over to him, wrapping one hand over his shoulder and lifting the gift up to him. "Take it."

He takes the gift and slowly unties the bow, then finds the seam to the foil and peels the tape, opening the wrapping just as I'd closed it, revealing the book in all its musty and faded glory. He doesn't say anything, just holds it in his hands, looking at it.

"I- I thought that with all your other books, you might like this. It's from my private collection."

He clears his throat. "I figured as much, this exact book costs lots of money and I'm pretty sure it wasn't easy for you to find. So why? Why would you give it to me?"

"It's something that I love, that tickles me pink, and that I thought you would appreciate. You're right, it wasn't easy to find. I searched for years, but then one day, when I wasn't even looking, just wandering around a used bookstore, I stumbled upon it. It was a very happy day. Sorta like how I've come to see finding you." I kiss his lips gently before walking back to the stove and turning it off. I pull the muffins from the oven and set them in a basket before plating everything else. I turn back and he hasn't moved.

"Are you okay?" I half-laugh.

He licks his lips, opens his mouth to start then stops, just looking at me, speechless. I look at him as if to say, well?

"I'm pretty sure, in an Angelically kind of way, you just told me you love me."

I put down his plate and mine, climbing up into my chair. "I just might have," I acquiesce, handing him his fork.

20

MAVERICK

DAY THIRTY-THREE, I NEVER ACTUALLY thought we'd see it after the second day we were together. We're still a bit like oil and vinegar at times, but we've survived. Today is going to be a long day for Angelica. Her daughter will be here next week and today, I've planned for her closest bandmate, Steve, and his wife to come for a visit. I figure we can cook out on the grill and kind of give Angelica a calm day after her therapy session.

After the doc left, Angelica went down to the stables. Apparently, whatever they discussed today was more than she wanted to deal with. I go about getting things ready for this afternoon and wait for her to come back to the house. I still need to tell her that Steve is coming.

I walk into my room to grab my tablet. I don't carry it around as much anymore. Angelica has been doing great work, so I give her a little more privacy. I always go back over everything at night after she goes to bed, but during the day, I make sure she doesn't need anything, then I usually head outside to read, or I work out.

I'm standing at my desk when I see movement out of the corner of my eye. I look up at my screen to see Angelica kissing Laurie. *What the actual fuck?* I suppose she's decided she doesn't want to wait to see if this can work or not. Not being able to watch any longer, I head for the counter facing the patio doors. This way, I'm the first thing Angelica sees when she walks through the door.

Leaning up against the counter, I watch for Angelica. She's been gone for a while and should be heading back this way any time now. I finally see her come through the doors, her boots in her hand, and my temperature is about boiling. She looks at me like a deer in headlights, she knows she's been caught without my saying a word.

"*Maverick*?" She drops her boots to the linoleum, her eyes fixed on me.

I watch her carefully to assess her, she's not giving me a damn thing at this point, just watching with wary eyes. "Have fun at the stables?" I finally spit at her.

"I… I don't know what you think you saw…" Angelica stammers.

"I know what I fucking saw. I don't know why I expected any less. I said we weren't ready and this pretty much puts the nail in the coffin," I growl.

"I didn't know she was here."

I stand up straight and throw my hand in the air to shut her up. "Bull. Fucking. Shit! She's here every Monday, Wednesday, and Friday because I knew those were the days you would most likely need to ride. God, aren't I a fucking idiot? Have you been fucking her this whole time? Did you find somewhere that I didn't have a camera?"

"*Fucking her?* I haven't even seen her since I've been back. This is the first time. She's usually gone before I get down there."

I shake my head and look at Angelica. I'm still spitting nails. "Okay, say it was your first time seeing her. Has everything this past month meant that fucking little to you? I mean I do things for a *reason*. I didn't have sex with you for the pure fact that you weren't ready and by God, I'm glad I didn't now. Why? Tell me that. Was I worth so little?"

"She kissed me, damn it! I didn't kiss her back. If you had watched a bit longer, you'd have seen that I shoved her ass to the ground."

"You wanted me to *keep watching*? *Seriously*? How could you even think I would be okay if I saw something like that? Wait, you were banking on the thought that I wouldn't be looking at that point, right? Well, guess what? I just happened to grab something off my desk when it happened. It's not like it matters. This is a job and I need to treat it that way." I grind my teeth and run a hand through my hair.

"Thirty-three days and counting, I think you broke the record," I hear a man say.

Turing, I see Steve, the drummer of Fallen Angels and Angelica's closest friend. "You can stop fucking counting cause I'm done. I lasted more than thirty days." I turn back to Angelica, "I was going to surprise you with company. *Surprise!* I'm fucking done with this bullshit. Bye. "

I storm passed Steve on the way to my room. I'm ready to pack my shit and get out of here. *This chick fucked with my head.* Slamming my door, I lean against it for a second before grabbing my suitcase and starting to pack my clothes. *Why her? What is it about her that just fucks me at all costs.* Placing the last of my jeans in the suitcase, I drop my head and run a hand over my face as my door swings open. I know it's Angelica, so I don't even look her way, just go back to grabbing clothes to pack.

"You've got a helluva lot of nerve." Angelica slams the door behind her. "Jealous rages on one hand, but I'm a fuckin' job on the other? You don't get it both ways!"

She's screaming now, so I just let her and keep packing. Not a lot for me to say at this point. Out of the corner of my eye, I see that she has moved deeper into the room.

"If I'm nothing more than a job to you then my indiscretion shouldn't matter. But I could've sworn declarations had been made and yet, you left me to blow the motor on my vibrator. So, excuse me if I was thrown by a little human contact."

I jerk my head to look at her. "You weren't ready! You're still not ready. Do you really think I haven't wondered what you'd feel like? I've wondered that same question and more since your second day home when you were in front of me, stark naked. *Jesus!*"

Angelica runs her hands through her hair and growls, "Where do you get off telling me what I am and am not ready for? It's my body. I know what it wants."

"Because I'm the fucking professional. You know what *your* body wants? Did your body want all the shit you've put into it? No! No one's body wants that. You did that because it made you forget and feel better for a short time. Sex is the same fucking way. I wasn't going to let you use me that way. You need to deal with your shit."

"What have I been doing here? What was I doing in

115

rehab? This isolation is making me even crazier. I need human touch." Angelica's voice cracks as she finishes.

"You want *sex* and you aren't ready," I say, trying to calm myself back down. With a shake of my head, I go back to packing.

Angelica grabs my wrist just as I put a shirt in my suitcase. "If all I wanted was sex, I could have had that an hour ago. Instead, I fired her."

"Good for you," I snap, ripping my wrist from her grasp and going for another shirt. Just as I've picked up a few more shirts, I hear a thud. Turning, I see my suitcase across the room, clothes on the bed and floor. "Are you fucking kidding me?" I shout.

"No, you do not get to tuck tail. I'm sorry if I don't fit in your little control bubble. Not ready? I'm not the one who's not ready here. You're so afraid of losing control that I don't think you'd know what to do with me if you got me."

I crash my mouth against Angelica's. Grabbing her ass tightly, I lift her just before I slam her into the door.

My cock is throbbing. I can't take her mouth anymore, I just need to shut her up.

21

ANGELICA

HIS MOUTH CRUSHES MINE, HIS HANDS grabbing my ass, lifting me up, and slamming me into the door. I guess I said the wrong thing, or perhaps the right thing, *finally*. He's given up his control. His hands slide up my back as he moans into my open mouth and tears open my top, sending buttons flying.

"Easy." I laugh.

"We've passed that," he growls, letting me down as my undershirt comes tearassing over my head. He turns me around, my face pressing against the door. The cold of it against my flushing skin feels good as I feel his nimble fingers unhook my bra and let it drop to the floor. He's got my tits in his hands firmly, his hard cock pressing against my ass through our jeans. I reach back, grabbing his head as he nips at my shoulder. I get a handful of his shirt, but he pushes me forward more, stopping to rip off his shirt, now I can feel his flesh against mine as he reaches into the waistband of my pants. *Fuck,* I wish I was better groomed for this. Razors do not do the job of Kylie, my waxer. I push back as he finds my hot button, giving it a tender swipe, and I moan. He leans into my ear and laughs, unzipping my pants, pushing them and my panties over my hips. With a guttural display, he spreads my thighs with his knee and I can hear his zipper as it drops.

"Uhh," I manage as he pushes deep into me, no priming, no warning prods. His thrusts are hard, fast, and needing. "Oh, God," I pant as I feel his sweat hitting my back. He pulls me toward him, getting deeper, and I clench up around him, coming, pressing my palms against the door. As I'm shaking, he pulls out of me and turns me around. I swear there's a twinkle in his eyes as he lifts me up and impales me once more, now pinning my back to the wall. My legs wrap his hips as he dives into me like the deep end of a pool.

I fish for a kiss and he obliges me as I feel him start to tighten up. He drops me onto the bed and grabs the closest thing to him, his T-shirt. Pulling out of me, he finishes before collapsing next to me. It wasn't romantic, or the best I've ever had, but fuck me, it was good and I want to do it again.

I curl up next to him, my leg wrapping over his as I kiss him. His chest is still heaving, poor guy did do all the work just now. "Please, don't leave me," I whisper. "I want you more than ever..." I reach down, stroking his cock. "This was our final hurdle and I'd say we just obliterated it."

Maverick runs a hand over his face. "I don't like how you make me question myself at every turn. I don't like being that way." I know he's referring to the loss of control he just had. "I *need* the control. Is what I like. It's how I've survived. You don't like to be controlled. How do you propose we overcome that?"

I crawl over so I'm sitting on top of him and

looking down into his eyes. "I'm not some wanton nymph. Hell, I've done nothing but be your willing slave since you've gotten here. What more control can I give you? Fetch you your slippers in my teeth?"

"I was actually here before you came home. Don't make me feel like I'm nothing. *Fuck,* don't make me question my sanity." Maverick places a hand on my cheek, pulling my face to his. "I don't like fighting with you, but moreover, I don't like feeling like I'm worth so little to you either. *I'm sorry.*"

This man has me twisted up in knots. What am I going to do with him? Staring down at him, I can feel my whole body want to melt into him. What has he done to me? "God, I wish you could see the doc's notes about you. You're all I think about, talk about, and I'm counting the days until you will let me break out of this house. I want to show you off, take you places, and take care of you. Just like you're taking care of me."

"I love you and you love me. We know this. Neither of us knows why in God's name fate decided we need to be together. Maybe she thought it'd be funny. When you think about it, this whole thing has been hilarious. Question is... How do we move on from here?"

There he is, Mister Control, he can't even bask in the afterglow for ten lousy minutes.

"Well," I smirk, "I've already got the big house and white picket fence. So, I'd say that we let love go and see where it takes us. Truthfully, I've never really been in love before. So far, I like it."

"Want a truth?" Maverick asks me.

"Of course."

"I've been in relationships, but never did I feel for any of them half of what I feel for you." Maverick runs his thumb in a circular motion on my cheek, making me smile.

"So, no leaving?"

"Apparently not, but you now get to do all this laundry." He points to all of his clothes around the room. I swear it's his entire wardrobe.

"I'm not the one who came in a T-shirt." I laugh.

"Better than inside or on *you*. You are the one who dumped my suitcase."

I look at Maverick with a pout on my face. "Fine, but it will have to be later because I have to go and entertain Steve, apparently." I kiss him on the forehead before sliding off him and bounding out the door.

Just as I'm on the other side, I hear, "Put some damn clothes on before going out there." I shake my head with a laugh. I wasn't planning to go out there naked. Knowing Steve, the kids are with him.

❊ ❊ ❊

I come out of the bedroom and everything is dead silent, but I can smell food before I even hit the kitchen. Steve's chopping one of the strongest onions on the planet, I fucking swear.

"Christ, Steve, what the hell? You're stinking up my damn house," I bemoan, covering up my mouth and nose.

"Yeah, well, it keeps the girls outta the house. Can't have um hearing all that was goin' on down the hall, now can we?" He lifts his brows at me, chopping hard on the board.

"I, um, well…" I cross my arms over my chest.

"It's alright, Queenie. From the sounds of it, you both needed it. I ain't one to judge." He wipes at his cheeks and sniffles. Onions are doing a right job on him too, he's a mess.

"What can I do to help? Usually, I do dinner."

He stops, looking me over like I've grown a third eye or something similarly ridiculous. "*You...* Cook?" He laughs.

"Yes, me. I'll have you know, I've always been able to cook, just didn't much have need to. Sheesh, Steve, you make me sound like some helpless little girl." I look everything over. The chopped sirloin is ready to be pressed into burgers and the steaks are already in marinade. Steve knows how to feed me, and there are salads too. Seems Crystal is lurking about as well, I spot her Ambrosia salad in the fridge as I grab water.

"If you say so. You should go out to the pool, the girls are down at the stables with the horses and Crystal, but Kellie is sprawled out on a lounger with a virgin daiquiri. Grab yourself one and join her, let us guys do the work for a change."

I watch him and he looks like he's in his element. Grilling is his thing, he likes to come here and take over and I like to let him. I nod and head for the patio.

"Hey, Queenie?" he calls after me and I stop, turning to him, my brow cocked in question. "If he hurts you, I'll bury him out in the desert and they'll never find the body."

Steve says the sweetest things.

22

MAVERICK

AFTER ANGELICA LEFT THE BEDROOM, I had a silent freak out. The pure fact that I control her and she likes it sent me over the deep end, but that mouth of hers is sending me straight to hell and quite possibly in a hand basket.

Steve was, as I expected, a prick, but with good reason. I've seen his relationship plenty of times, but there is something going on with him and his wife, Kellie. Crystal, their girlfriend, is tense. Either she knows what's going on between the couple or she senses it. Apparently, one of the girls is away. They didn't really talk about it much when Angelica asked about her. Steve's youngest two sure had a blast. They were always watching me, giggling. From what everyone said they only do that with Brent, one of the other members of the band. The whole family could use a therapist.

Dinner went over smoothly, but Angelica and I didn't talk a lot after everyone left. I busied myself, quickly gathering my clothes and cleaning them. I should have made Angelica do it, but she had enough to do with her daughter coming in two days. We both slept in our own beds, which I think is for the best.

I wake to the smell of bacon and something else but can't figure out what it is. I go about getting myself ready so I can go see what she's up to. Walking into the kitchen, her back is to me while she's at the stove, so I just lean up against the wall and watch her.

Angelica has taken on her cooking role really well. Right now, watching and listening to her hum and sing as she cooks is cute. It's a softer side that I don't usually get to see. Angelica turns and notices I'm standing here. A smile sweeps across her face.

"What are you standing there all creepy like for?"

"I smelled food and it woke me. Then I get in here and your humming and singing. I was pleasantly surprised," I answer, walking over and sitting down.

As she watches me, I can see the worry in her eyes. "So, what do we got to do today?"

"I have stuff that should be delivered today for Angela's room, but other than that, we need to get the rooms set up. Probably need to get you on the computer at some point, so you can order her a few gifts. Maybe make gift baskets or something for Janice and Alec... Just what I've been thinking."

Angelica's eyes dart back and forth as she takes in everything I just said. "Gift baskets? I wouldn't even know what to put in them. Not for those two. I mean, I don't really know much about them. I just know they take care of my girl and she doesn't complain."

"How about I worry about the gift baskets, but you have to pick out gifts for the kid."

She nods, blowing out air. "I think I can handle that much." She's nervous, I can see it in her micro-movements, every muscle is on edge.

"So today, on top of getting everything ready for Saturday, we still have meal prep. I really think we should keep you on your meal plan, but I can order anything we need for the others. Are we doing the gym, tennis, or basketball today?"

"I don't really care. I just need something to do today. Give me something to focus on," Angelica snaps.

"Then let's have breakfast and you can pick what you want to do. I have to step away right after breakfast for a phone call."

Angelica nods her head and begins plating food. We eat in silence; this place has that eerie silence right now. I know it's because I'm not quite ready to talk about yesterday yet. Mainly because I have to speak with Christy. I'm already lying by omission by not telling him. Therefore, talking about it with Angelica is just not possible right now.

After breakfast, I prepare for the call with Christy, the band's manager. He calls right at nine on the dot. I think he may be worse than I am. I update him on everything going on. He has no clue about Angela, which isn't surprising. Angelica is a private person, but where do I have any room to talk? Christy wants me to do another get together with more of the band. I'll need to call Steve for help with that since I haven't met any of them other than Ringo and Steve. Before hanging up, I am told to keep him updated on the daughter.

Now I sit here waiting for Steve to answer his phone while watching Angelica in the kitchen through the cameras.

"Yo?" Steve answers.

"Hello, Steve, this is Maverick."

"Maverick, hi. What can I do you for?" Steve asks with a chuckle.

"Well, I just got off the line with Christy. Seems he wants Angelica to get together with more of the band. So, that led me to call you, as I've only met you and Ringo thus far."

"Oh, yeah? Well, that leaves you with the Brothers Grimm."

"Explain?"

"You've got Brent, who is neurotic at best and a train wreck at his worst. He's also got a very pregnant and headstrong wife, who also happened to knock out some of Angelica's teeth. Then, on the other hand, you have Kyle, her enabler."

"Fuck." My knees start to shake. "What's Ringo's story?"

"Ringo? He's the glue that holds us all together."

I run a hand down my face and let out a long sigh. "Could this band be any more fucked up?"

"We did meet in rehab."

"All of you?" Fuck! My job just got a billion times harder.

"Me, Angelica, and Brent. I used to ride the H train."

"I know Angelica's addictions. What's Brent's?"

"Brent? Booze, coke, pills, whatever he can get his hands on. He's been sober for a while now. There have been slips here and there. The last time, Angelica tried to take advantage of it. Which is why there's tension between them. When she's high, she's not the best person. When she's clear... Well, you've seen that."

"You've got your stuff, Brent's an addict, Ringo's hiding something from everyone, and since you've said Kyle is the enabler, he's still on the drugs. Just fucking grand. What in God's name did I get myself into?"

Steve laughs. "Well, two choices, my man. Swing

for the fences or call in a pinch hitter."

"Right now, I want to say fuck Christy, but I can't. I've got a ball of nerves in the kitchen because her daughter will be here in two days and is staying for a week. Now, I have to host a fucking get together and hope and pray it goes better than the last one. Sorry about all that by the way."

"Hey, you had a few kinks that needed to be worked out. Who am I to judge?"

"It wasn't very professional of me and I'm sorry for that." I glance over the cameras to see Angelica cleaning up the porch. "I suppose let's go Ringo, Brent, and his wife. I really don't think she can handle Kyle yet. Let me know what day's good for you and I'll schedule it in."

"Well, with Angela coming, do you want to do this when she's here or after she leaves? I can bring the girls for her to play with."

"Christy wants it done ASAP. I do think we need to let her get adjusted. Are you all doing anything for the Fourth?"

"My thoughts exactly. We were gonna go to Brent's, but I can make him adjust that."

"Hot dogs and hamburgers, or do you all eat something else?" I ask Steve.

"Hot dogs, hamburgers, steak, ribs, whatever you want to do. We'll all bring something."

"Great. Just shoot me a text with what everyone's bringing and I'll get the rest. As for the kids, um, what do they like to do?" I pull the phone away from my ear as Steve laughs and I know it must be shaking him with how loud he is. "*What*?"

"I'm sure they'll amuse themselves. Weren't you ever a little kid?" Steve laughs again before hanging up.

What the fuck have I gotten myself into? I look for

Angelica and can't find her on the screen, so I check the time. I've been in my room all morning and it's closing in on one o'clock. Standing, I head to Angelica's room. The door's shut, so I knock and wait for an answer.

Angelica doesn't answer, so I test the knob and the door opens. I find her sitting on the bed with her head in her hands. I walk over and squat down in front of her, placing my hands on her legs. "What's going on in that head of yours?"

Angelica sniffs and I can tell she's been crying. "I can't stop my head from racing. I thought a shower would help, but I'm just all over the place. I'm terrified of Angela showing up."

"That's to be expected. What if we curl up in the bed and I just hold you for a while? Maybe it will help you calm down."

Angelica nods her head and scoots herself up the bed. Slipping off my shoes, I climb in beside her. Laying down, I pull her into me and with her head on my chest, I wrap my arms around her.

"Thank you." She rubs my chest softly.

"What are you thanking me for?" I stay her hand, holding it against me.

"Finally opening up to me. Even if only just a little."

"Oh, Cupcake, we still have a long way to go."

Angelica smiles up at me before reaching up to kiss me.

"Woah, you've got a lot going on in that head of yours. Let's dial it back a notch and deal with everything else before going there. I need to make sure your head is in the right place."

With a shake of her head, she looks away. "It was just a kiss. If I wanted *more*, I'd be in your lap."

"Kissing leads to more."

Angelica sits up and moves down the bed in rapid irritation. "You know what? I can't just sit here. I think I'm gonna go for a run."

"No," I state. "You need to stay where you are. I need to get a better vibe coming off you before you're off doing something else, because if I can't get you calm, I will be putting everything off. Instead of anyone staying here, I will put them up in the best hotel. Right now, the only thing that matters is your well-being."

Angelica looks at me with contempt, rolling her shoulders back defiantly as she stares at me. "I can't just sit here idle. I need to be doing something."

"We are. I'm holding you and you're talking, which is exactly where you need to be." My voice takes a deeper, more domineering tone. Sometimes it takes a bit more control.

Angelica watches me and is becoming very twitchy, she's about to bolt. I grab her, pinning her to the bed as I straddle her ribs with just enough pressure to keep her from fighting me. "I told you *no*. Damn it, I mean what I say. I will cancel everything."

"Cancel it!" she screams. "At this point, what the fuck do I care? It'll save me from fucking it all up." Tears are streaming down her face as she glares up at me.

"If you didn't care, we wouldn't be here. Now would we?" Angelica's sobs shake her under me. "Do you not want to see your daughter? Do you not want to be able to walk out of this house? Tell me, why throw away all the progress we've made because you're scared?"

"Because I don't know what else to do." She breaks eye contact.

"I'm right here and have been for thirty-four days.

I'm not going anywhere." I soften my voice, her crying is gonna break me.

"But *how* are you going to be here?"

"The same way I have been, and when I know you're really ready, hopefully, more. I told you we still have a long way to go."

"The problem is I'm going to need more *now*. At least this week. I'm going to need more than the counseling. I need someone *by my side* now, not someone standing over my shoulder." She looks at me with pleading eyes.

"I'll be right beside you every step of the way. I'm not letting you do any of it alone."

"What if she doesn't like me?" Angelica whimpers.

"How could she not?"

"I've never been completely sober around her. I was the mom who was fun because I got high. I was fearless, always up for adventures... Now, I don't know who I am."

"Who do you think you are?" She doesn't realize the incredible woman she is, all that she's accomplished in so short a time.

"That's just it, I don't *know*. I don't know who I'm supposed to be now."

"Who do you want to be?"

"I wanna be somebody you don't have to hold down."

"You'll get there, but you have to walk before you can run. You also can't run every time something freaks you out." I ease up on her, sitting back and she just lays there, defeated.

"Old habits die hard. I'm sorry."

"I get that, but at the same time, you aren't trying to run."

"Where would I go?"

"You tell me."

"The only place would be a place I don't want to be. I don't want to end up at the bottom of another bottle… Of any kind."

"I know you've talked about this with the doc, but the only person who can change *that* is *you*. The doc, me, your daughter, your band… None of us can help with that. It has to be all you." Angelica nods her head. "So, how about we do as I suggested and cuddle for a bit and calm down your racing mind?"

"I can *try*."

I smile at Angelica then take my place beside her. I cuddle her in my arms as she lays her head on my chest once more. After a while, I hear soft breathing, Angelica has fallen asleep. She snuggles in closer and I tighten my hold on her because right now, she just needs the reassurance.

23

ANGELICA

TWILIGHT IS SETTLING IN WHEN I WAKE, still in Maverick's arms. I have half a mind to wake him with kisses, but he stalled me the last time I tried to start something, so instead, I slip from the bed, leaving him sleeping soundly. Fuck, I'm in relationship limbo with him, but there isn't much I can do about it, not right now at least. There's too much more going on, my little girl will be here in less than forty-eight hours. What I want right now is a fucking drink, that would settle me, or a bit of Vicodin. I feel twitchy, like those first few days in rehab. My mouth is dry and my bones hurt, my skin feels like it's gonna slough off and run away.

I watch Maverick for a few moments, he looks so peaceful. Wish I could sleep that deep and not toss and turn with nightmares like I do most nights. It's a good thing he doesn't have cameras in here or he'd see. See that I'm still not as right as rain, as they say. Cold sweats, hot flashes, muscle aches, yet every morning I get up. I soldier on. I have to, and yet I wonder too. Wonder if it's all worth it, wonder if I still want the same things I did when I went into rehab. I've spent the last two months sequestered from the world. It's easy to stay clean when you don't have *access*, but what am I going to do once I'm back in the world? Am I strong enough to say no? Right now, I'm not so sure, and that scares the shit outta me. If I slip, will I lose him? I mean one meaningless kiss was almost enough, but if I fuck up and wind up high, then what? Will he understand? Does he have the capacity to *forgive*?

He turns over and settles deeper into the pillows and I grab my sneakers and am out of the bedroom, making a beeline for the front door. I don't know where I'm going, I just know I need air, I need to breathe, because right now I'm choking, the walls are closing in on me. I should have woken him up, but I can't deal with his watchful eyes right now. I need to learn ways to cope by *myself*. I swing the door open and slam right into a stack of boxes at the threshold. Ouch, that fucking hurt! Rubbing my knee, I count more than a dozen boxes, some of them really big, but relatively light, to my surprise. This must be the stuff he ordered for Janice, Alec, and my baby girl. The gate guard left the dolly. I sigh and start to stack the boxes, at least it gives me something to do.

❧ ❧ ❧

It took me about thirty minutes to get it all inside and laid out. He ordered new bedding for their bedrooms, better sheets, comforters, there's enough to change the bedding like three times for Angela! What does he think, she's gonna mess it up or something? I shake my head with a laugh. He bought the newest video game systems, or rather, *I* bought. He is doing all of this with my accounts after all. The thing is, I have a full game room, or I did until he emptied it out as part of my earning trust and privileges. I'm something of a closet gamer. Love those RPG fantasy games, I have hundreds of games, going all the way back to the old-school Nintendo system. Hell, I even have an Atari for nostalgia.

They were always good for when I was hermitting, or just high enough to still make sense of the storylines, and with the newest ones, they are so well drawn, who wouldn't fall in deep? I miss my games. Maverick ordered the newer systems, but no games. I guess he is fixin' to go out and get them maybe? That would be nice, I would love to get out of this house, if only for a little while. Maybe have an excuse to put on something other than my bum around or gym clothes. I earned my heels back, but what's the point of wearing them around the house?

I decide that since I've still seen hide nor hair of Maverick that I'll take to setting up the two rooms. That will keep me busy while my shrimp boil cooks. I'm feeling like something spicy.

I think I'm gonna have him pick up some crawdads for the holiday. I remember Angela and I had a helluva time shuckin' and suckin' them down, must have gone through a pound each with corn on the cob and piles of curly peppered fries. That was the last weekend I saw her, a year ago. I was chugging beers and if it hadn't been for Jake, my then body guard, I don't think we'd have made it home in one piece, I was so lit. Janice flipped on me, Alec threatened to not let me see her again unless I pulled my shit together, but I was so fucked up again that I didn't listen. Then the band blew up, we started touring and I just didn't have the time for her. Is that what's going to happen again? Even sober, the road calls, it will take me away for months at a time. What do I do if Alec and Janice are here for more than just a weekend?

Am I prepared to take on my little girl in a full-time capacity? If he's really sick, it's a possibility this is more than a visit. They've never adopted her, only taken on partial guardianship for legal purposes so I could hide her. All it would take is a few scratches of ink on paper and the agreement would be dissolved, and Angela would be all mine again.

I put Janice and Alec in the dove gray room, the bedding is all neutral, so it won't clash, and this room has a sunrise view of the mountains. I think they will like it. They've never been here before. I always go to them, me, one bodyguard, and a single suitcase and carry on. It was always easier that way. It kept me reminded that she belonged where she was, and I had places to be. I *love* my girl, but sometimes, looking at her, I see her father in her mannerisms and it takes me to dark places. I've never spent extended periods of time with her, not since I had her. The music kept me busy, kept me away. The drugs kept me from caring, from missing her too terribly. Sober? I ache for her even as I fear seeing her. Doc Peters knows how I feel and she just says that I need to stand firm, remember that I am her *mother* and that all I've done, however misguided, including staying away, was for her, for her protection, and born out of love. I only hope she's right because right now, all I feel is dread.

I look around the pink room. It's the southern facing bedroom and just one removed from my own. Close enough to get to her, but far enough away that my thin walls are not an issue. I sometimes wake up sobbing loudly. How Maverick hasn't heard me in all this time, I may never know. The full-size bed is covered with a white comforter with oversized, brightly colored daisies all over it. It's sweet, I'm not sure how my nine-year-old is gonna feel about it, but hopefully, she's at least polite if she doesn't like it.

I hang the new curtains, which are color blocked to match the comforter, and fluff up the pillows, placing the big white teddy bear with a pink nose in the center. Aside from the gaming systems, Maverick also got this massive bear. I don't know how they will get it on the plane, the thing is gonna need its own suitcase! Looking around, I notice that all the furniture in this room is light oak, it is, by far, the brightest room in my house. I think I may have subconsciously decorated it for Angela. I smile to myself, proud that I managed so much in so little time, and put the horses out too. I even hooked the video games up with the splitter box Maverick was perceptive enough to realize we'd need.

It's going on eight fifteen when the food finishes and I plate it all up, putting it on a tray. Last time I looked in on Maverick, he'd pulled my blanket over his head. If he's gonna sleep in here tonight, it's fine by me, but the boy hasn't eaten since breakfast and I busted my ass, so he's gonna get up and have his chow.

I go into the room and sure enough, he's still under cover. Letting out a short laugh, I put down the food on my dresser and climb into the bed, wiggling under the blanket and back into his arms.

"*Maverick*? Wake up, I've got food," I whisper, tracing his jaw line with my in desperate need of a manicure nail. He and I need to talk about having someone come out tomorrow, as I need a haircut too and I don't wanna see my girl *ungroomed*.

"Maverick?" I say a bit louder, my lips just inches from his.

"Hmm, I'm awake, what time is it?" he asks with closed eyes. His glasses fell off at some point and I have no idea where they are.

"It's almost eight -thirty." I smile.

He's rubbing his face, nearly hitting me. "Why'd you let me sleep so long?"

I snuggle against him closer, my leg sliding up his. "You looked peaceful and I had stuff to do."

"You shouldn't have let me sleep…"

I shake my head with a short laugh. "You looked too comfy to bother, besides, I made dinner, set up the bedrooms for our would-be company, and took care of the horses too."

He's got that groggy, sleepy face as he attempts to sit up, looking around for his glasses. "What'd you make?"

"A shrimp boil, wanted something spicy."

"Okay, you seen my glasses?"

I go to help him, searching the covers, and at last, I find them, sliding them onto his face with a grin as I sit up on my knees and kiss him softly.

"Hmm… Much better, I can see everything again."

I slide off the bed, deflected once again. "I don't understand why you don't just wear contacts or better yet, just get Lasik." I grab the food and turn back to him.

"Tried contacts, don't like um, they feel funny. As for surgery, why? My glasses work just fine, had um for damn near twenty-five years."

"You're lucky you're adorkable." I put the food down and climb back into bed.

"Pretty positive that's not a word." He opens his foil packet.

"Sure, it is, it's a hybrid of adorable and dork. Let's face it, *these*," I touch the side of his glasses, "make you look like a college professor."

"And that means what?"

"I get to play the naughty freshman after dinner?" I smirk, popping a shrimp into my mouth.

"Is that all you ever think about, woman? I mean, sheesh, can't a man even wake up?"

"Wake up all you like, and eat up too. There's more in the kitchen, I kinda went overboard." I smile sheepishly.

"Thought we talked about you not being alone?"

"I had Lucille, she followed me around, kept me company. I do need to learn to cope on my own."

"Yes, maybe, but you're still supposed to have me with you."

"And if I had, I wouldn't have been alone, now eat, or I'm gonna be forced to feed you myself."

"And if I take you up on that offer?"

My eyes slide in his direction. Is he teasing me? I put my plate aside and grab his from in front of him, climbing into his lap. I take a forkful of food and bring it up to his mouth. "I'll drop an article of clothes for every bite you take."

"But that doesn't get our work done, does it?" He smiles, his hands on my waist.

"What's left to do today, other than chow and play?" I wiggle on top of him.

"Um, I ordered a bunch of stuff?" his voice rises to a higher pitch.

"Yeah, all the bedding, video games, and toys. I already hooked it all up." I smirk as he takes the bite from the fork. One down, I unbutton the first few buttons on my top, revealing a black bra and plenty of cleavage.

"It seems you've been busy today." He takes another bite and I slip the top off completely.

"That's what I've been saying." I let the top fall to the floor. "But I've still got a bit of pent up energy, you gonna help me expend it?" I ask, offering him another bite.

He takes it, his grip on my sides tightening. I know I'm torturing him, but given how long he's made me wait, turnabout is fair play. I unsnap my bra and let it drop between us, he breathes hard through a sigh.

"You're the devil," he whispers. "You're the devil and I'm going straight to Hell." He grabs me by the back of the head and pulls me to him, kissing me.

24

MAVERICK

SHE SMELLS LIKE THE HORSES, BUT HER KISS is full of spice. This is gonna get messy if I don't get creative fast. I lift her, getting off the bed, and her legs wrap over my hips as her bare chest presses against me. She sighs into my ear as I carry her into the bathroom before putting her down. She's panting and looking around, confused.

"We don't have condoms and I'm not using my shirt *again*." I chuckle, turning on the water in the massive shower. When I turn toward her again, she's almost on top of me, grabbing my shirt and ripping it up over my head. I swear she is getting bolder, gonna need to nip that, right quick. I halt her attempted assault of my mouth and she bites her lip with yearning.

"Take off those pants, I can still smell the horses on you," I order. She smirks, stepping back and undoing her jeans. They peel down over her hips to reveal a black pair of boy shorts. Fuck me, she's sexy as all hell. I adjust my stance, my hardon getting uncomfortable, as I crook a finger at her.

HANEY/HAYES

She knows what she needs to do. Like a jungle cat, she hits all fours and crawls to me. Getting up on her knees, she unbuttons my pants with her teeth, a smile teasing at the sides of her mouth. Running my hand through her hair and along her face, I watch as she drops my boxer briefs and puts my cock into her beautifully hot and wet mouth. I lean back against the shower door as she works me with her tongue, her head bobbing back and forth in delicious rhythm. I know I should stop her, I know this is all her way of deflecting the things that she needs to talk about, but right now, my cock just needs to be buried inside her again.

Grabbing her by the wrists, I pick her up and she lets out a gasp when I kiss her hard and deep, wrangling her panties off and dragging her into the shower with me. I have her pinned to the wall as the hot water streams down over us and I break into her, finally ripping a loud and satisfied moan from my own chest. God help me, she feels so good wrapped around me as I pound into her and her nails bite into my shoulder blades. I wince, which makes her chuckle.

"I- know I need-a- manicure," she gasps between my thrusts. "Think we could call someone to handle it?" Her lips tease mine.

"Whatever you want, just shut up and fuck me." What the hell am I saying? She starts pushing against the wall, slamming her little body against me as she comes. I like the feel of her body sliding against mine, it pushes me over the edge and I pull from her, about to come. She hits her knees once more, taking my cock back into her mouth, sucking me until not a drop is left in me. I pick her up and wash her down, the scent of orchids and honey fills the room from her body wash and gets me hard all over again.

"Hmm, seems I've got another round in me," I say as she rinses the conditioner from her hair with an eye raise.

"Good thing there's hot water left." She wraps her arms around my neck as I pin her to the wall once more.

* * *

This morning has been all kinds of fucked up. To start, I was woken up by Angelica in my bed. I about fucking squashed her. She told me she couldn't sleep. I've always told her she could wake me. To make matters worse, she was fucking stark naked. I wanted to take her right there in my bed, but I didn't. Her daughter comes *today* and we need to be up and ready for them to get here. Angelica is supposed to be heading to the kitchen after she cleans herself up.

Flipping the lock on my door, I kick off my briefs and head straight for the bed. My cock is hard and fucking aching. I get comfortable in bed and grip my fist around my cock. With a deep breath in and out, I stroke as slowly as I can manage. There's not much use in trying to draw it out, though. Angelica fucks with my head daily and seeing her in my bed, naked, has sent me over the edge. Her creamy skin, nipples pert and darker than most women's, combined with the look on her face damn near leveled me. Remembering the look she gets as she comes has me groaning in my own release, hot, thick jets of cum coating my chest.

Heading for the shower, I clean myself up because there will be a knock at my door shortly. Breakfast doesn't usually take her very long. After my shower, I go through my natural routine of getting dressed and brushing my teeth. Except this time, I also have to change the sheets on my bed.

Before a knock can come to the door, I'm heading for the kitchen and watching Angelica plate what she's made. Since Angela show's up today, Angelica and I need to have ourselves a talk. Walking over to Angelica, I kiss her on the head, then take my seat.

"Breakfast smells good."

Angelica touches her forehead and looks at me, confused. "Did we miss a step this morning?"

I glance around like I'm looking for something. "Not that I know of." Angelica rubs a hand down her cheek and chin, watching me with a smile. "Are you okay? Got something on your face?"

"No, but *you* certainly do," Angelica says, putting my plate in front of me.

"Oh, I thought I'd try it out. Whatcha think?"

"I think I'm allergic to it, so it's going to have to go."

With a roll of my eyes, I chuckle. "Okay, I will take care of it right after breakfast."

As we sit here eating, I try to figure out how to talk to Angelica. I've slept in her bed with her in my arms and now she's been in my bed more than once. Does she expect it to happen all the time? Just when she wants? I enjoy having her with me, but it seems like it's far too soon for that. It's too soon for sex too, but that won't be stopping now that it's started. Having her tight, wet, and wrapped around me is damn near heaven in disguise. Thinking about that, I really need to order some fucking condoms and get her on some form of birth control. My shirts just aren't going to work and I *don't* want kids.

"So, I think we need to talk a bit before company shows up."

"Oh? I don't like that sound of that." Angelica stops

mid-bite while watching me.

"I'm going to set you up with your gyno doctor. It's about time you get on birth control."

Angelica's mouth pops open and her brow raises. "Good luck with that."

"No luck needed. It's either that or there's no more sex for us. I'm ordering condoms, but we need more protection than just those," I say before putting another bite in my mouth.

"The problem is birth control makes me sick."

"All of them?" I look at her, astonished.

"The handful that I've *tried*. It's the hormones that are in them."

Dropping my fork, I rub my hands through my hair and down my face before placing them on the back of my head. "How, pray tell, do you expect to not get pregnant then?" I ask, never looking up.

I hear the telltale sign of heels clicking on the floor just before Angelica's hand is on my shoulder. I look up into her blue eyes and I know she can see the tension all over my face.

"Maverick, I've been having sex since I was fourteen. Obviously, condoms work. So, unless you're Superman and your sperm goes faster than a speeding bullet, I think we'll be alright."

I watch her watching me. What she said should calm me, but it's not doing anything of the sort. I'll let it go for now and just keep pulling out even with the condoms. Even just to keep my own sanity. "Okay, but we still have something else to figure out."

Angelica takes a step back and crosses her arms over her chest. "Okay?"

It's then I notice just how she's dressed. A pair of fitted black Capris, with an off the shoulder short sleeve top, her freshly cut hair gelled back, and her makeup perfect with cherry red lips that match her four-inch heels. I've never seen her dressed like this, she looks good though. Man, do I feel like I'm not dressed up enough, but I'm not changing clothes. I wear what I wear and that isn't changing. "The sleeping in each other's bed. Is that supposed to be happening all the time? I mean your daughters coming, maybe we should cool it till she's gone?"

Angelica blinks slowly, then scoff at me. "I don't see what difference that makes and I wasn't really looking to make a habit of it anyway since it freaked you out. Don't worry, I'll stay in my room like a good little girl. *Sir*."

"That's not what I meant. Damn it! You haven't seen her in a year. You need to focus on that and not this." I motion between the two of us. "I wouldn't have flipped my shit had I not almost squashed you like a fucking bug. Jesus Christ. If you want to sleep in there, do it. Just let me know you are there, so I don't roll over on you." Angelica's looking at me and clicking her tongue. "I know I don't say shit right, but give me a break. You're *difficult*. I'm still trying to train myself not to ask the questions or do the shit I'd naturally do in the position I'm in."

"I've told you before, ask me what you will. I don't have anything to hide from you. As for this," she motions between the two of us, mimicking me, "if my daughter cares enough to ask, I'm just going to tell her that you're Mommy's boyfriend. If that's alright by you? Because frankly, anything else would be confusing."

I watch her quietly and sit back in my chair. She wants to tell the kid that I'm her *boyfriend*, which is what we said I am, but won't that confuse the kid? I mean we sleep in different rooms. Me being who I am, I ask those exact questions. "Won't that confuse her? Us in different rooms?"

"Hell, I don't know. It's not like we're married. We're not Alec and Janice. I don't even know if she'll notice."

"I don't know much on the subject of kids, but I know they pick up on more than they should. No, we aren't married, but we live under the same roof, which is more than most couples."

Angelica wraps her arms around my neck with a sly smile on her face. "Then I guess you're going to be shacking up with me for the next week since I have the bigger bed."

"Now don't go getting ahead of yourself. Angela may want to sleep in there with you."

"Now, wait a minute, you can't unring that bell." Angelica laughs just as the doorbell rings.

25

ANGELICA

THEY'RE HERE. The sound of the doorbell ringing brings me and my playing to a halt and I'm suddenly stiff as a board, terror and doubt rushing back into me.

Maverick wraps his arms around me, kissing me softly before whispering, "You can do this, I have faith in you."

I swallow hard, looking into his deep blue eyes that command me so easily, hoping for an ounce of his strength. He nods at me as his hands leave my waist and he turns me to the door.

"Go on, now. I'm right here with you."

I take a breath and he takes my hand, letting me lead him to the front door. It rings a second time as we reach it and I pull it open to face Janice. She's shorter than me, all of five feet one, five feet four in her heels, which like me, she usually can't be caught without. Her blonde hair is down to her shoulders and in soft waves that frame sparkly blue eyes. I furrow my brow now to look at her, though, she looks tired and it's only nine a.m.

"Janice?" I ask as she smiles, hugging me.

"Hello, girl." She laughs, though it feels forced to me. "It's good to see you. You look well." Her hug is tentative, obviously for show, though I don't know if it's for Maverick or for Angela. Our last encounter wasn't pleasant, so I don't rightly blame her.

"Thank you, you too," I *lie*. Looking around her, I see that the driver is unloading baggage and Alec is just now opening the back door. Janice and I separate. My mouth is dry. Little feet pop out first, covered by pink flip-flops with purple toenail polish. Angela appears in white jean shorts and a pink tank top with white trim. I can feel the tears welling up already, her hair is almost passed her shoulders and it's in a ponytail. She's looking everywhere but at me.

"She's gotten so big," I whisper, stepping outside.

"Yeah, growing like a weed," Janice quips. "Angie, come see your momma."

Angie? *Really*? I give her a beautiful name and they drop it to something so *generic*? Angela looks toward the doors and smiles when her eyes rest on me. In seconds, she's in my arms and I'm a mess.

"I barely have to bend to kiss her face, she's gotten so tall," I say to Alec as he comes up the walk.

"Seems she's taking after the *father*?" he mumbles, coming to stand beside Janice. Dick. He would say something like that. Ugh, I'm not letting it get to me. I'll let it wash passed me and focus on my girl. My beautiful Angela.

"I've missed you," I say, still hugging her.

"I missed you too, Mommy." She laughs as I cover her with kisses. *Mommy*? It feels good to hear her call me that. Really good.

"Come on in, guys, the driver will bring your stuff

in and we can get you set up, your rooms are ready. Have you eaten? I can fix something if you are hungry."

"We're fine, a little tired if anything," Alec answers.

"Oh? Sure, let us get you to your room, and you can rest."

"I'm not tired," Angela breaks in.

"Then you don't have to lie down," I say with a smile. "You can hang out with us."

"*Us?*" Angela asks curiously.

"Christ, I nearly forgot." I laugh, looking up and seeing Maverick simply watching me interact. "Guys, this is Maverick."

"Yes, we've spoken a few times." Janice smiles, putting out her arms and hugging him. He's stiff about it but takes it in stride. Alec sees his tension and instead of the hug, goes for the handshake, which goes more smoothly.

Angela walks over to him, one hand on her hip and the other on her chin as though she's considering him like a piece of artwork. She looks him up and down and then walks around him.

Maverick stands perfectly still, not sure what to do, I think. As she examines him, an awkward smile takes over his face.

"Hmm, I guess he'll do for piggy back rides later." She smiles, coming back over to me and taking my hand. "Have I got my own room?"

"Yup." I laugh, making a confused face at Maverick who just rubs his hands over his face, then makes a shaving motion. I nod as he makes his way to his room.

❄ ❄ ❄

I talked Maverick into watching Angela in the pool

while Janice and I start lunch. I'm making taco salads with ground turkey and I'm being ambitious by actually making the tortilla bowls, deep frying them in coconut oil. The kitchen smells delicious! Janice is chopping tomatoes while I handle the peppers and cheeses. I can hear Angela laughing and trying to goad Maverick into joining her in the water, which makes me smile.

"He seems like a nice man," Janice finally speaks up. "He's certainly got you moving in the right direction."

I nod, looking at her. I noticed that she and Alec packed light compared to Angela and it has me filled with questions. Questions I'm not sure I'm ready to have the answers for just yet. "He does," I finally answer. "He's been good for me, but I'm also serious about staying clean this time."

"That's good to hear." She sighs. "Listen, I'm not one to beat around the bush and small talk is for candy asses, so I may as well come out with it." She doesn't stop what she's doing, but her tone is super serious.

"He's not as well as he looks, is he?" I ask straightly.

She shakes her head and I see her choke back her tears. "The doctors say that if he doesn't respond to treatment, he has about a year."

"Janice, I'm sorry. What can I do? I mean, if it's about money-"

"No, his insurance is good, the mill is taking care of us, they even raised the extra cash for what the insurance wouldn't pay for. This is about Angie."

There it is. I knew this was more than just a visit, their coming out here means something far more. They are assessing me.

"Angelica, the reality is that I can't take care of a

sick husband and handle *your* little girl. I love her, but she needs someone who will be there for her, someone who can be patient with her. Christ, he's barely sick and I'm already losing my shit." She wipes a tear from her face and puts the knife down hard. "I hit her! The other day, she was just playing outside and I had warned her not to get too dirty because we were headed out to the market, but she skidded in the grass and scuffed up her pants. I had been in the house dealing with Alec's nausea again and when I came out and saw, I lost it. She tried to explain what happened, but her mouth runnin' just set me off and I hit her right in the face." She's sobbing, looking at the counter.

"You're stressed, I'm sure you didn't mean to do it," I try to console her, but she shirks from my touch. "I don't know what I'd do in your position."

"I just can't... She's got a mouth on her, no matter what we try and do, she argues or tries to negotiate, constantly. From what's for supper to her bedtime and homework, it feels like a constant battle. It was cute at first and I know it's our fault for spoiling her, but what were we to do? Keep what you sent from her? Every penny you've ever given us has gone to her in some fashion. She has the best clothes, toys, goes to a great school. What more could she want?"

"I've never denied that you take very good care of her. It's why she's with you. I don't understand what you want from me though."

"You're sober now." Janice sniffles. "Don't you want her? I mean for more than a day or two?"

"I wouldn't know where to start."

"She loves you, she talks about you constantly, has all your music, even the stuff from when you were with *Blues Country*. She wants to be with you."

I shake my head, that feeling of dread filling me up. Maverick has made it sorta clear that he doesn't really do kids. I mean not in those words to me, but his way of speaking and his being so adamant about me not getting knocked up make his point for him. What would my taking her do to us? I look outside and he's still on the edge of the pool while she swims alone.

"I- I don't know that I could. You know how often and how long I am on the road." I finally come up with a reasonable excuse.

"I also know that your drummer has kids and that they are frequently with you. You've said so yourself. So, you take her along. She's dying to get out of Louisiana. The honest truth is that we don't plan on bringing her home with us if we don't have to."

My eyes bug out of my head. "What? I mean, you're just gonna abandon her here?"

"It's not abandonment, it's doing what's best for my family and for her. I don't trust myself not to lash out at her again. Do you want me to hurt her? Even if it's only an accident? Then the child protective services would come in and we'd lose her to the system. I'd never forgive myself. You'd never forgive me. Angelica, you've hidden her away, and hidden from her for nine years. It's time you step up and be a mom because that little girl, she needs you." Janice stands up, walking toward the bedrooms, no doubt to check on her husband and let him know she's laid out their plans into my fragile little lap.

26

MAVERICK

THIS WEEKEND HAS BEEN LONG, especially with a kid scrutinizing every damn thing I do. I've made sure to keep a tablet on me at all times to make notes on how Angelica is handling everything. Plus, I'm sleeping in her bed while Angela is here. Something's on her mind though, and I don't like the fact that she isn't telling me what.

It's Sunday night and I've just finished with my shower since Angelica was saying goodnight to Angela. I'm in bed, reading *Dead Until Dark* by Charline Harris. I've been meaning to read this one for a while because friends have been giving me shit about never watching True Blood. Fuckers just don't understand I can't watch something knowing it's a book.

Angelica walks into the room and I glance up, then back to my book. "So, what's your assessment, professor?"

Placing the book on my chest, I look at her with a cocked brow. "Assessment of what?"

"My daughter," Angelica says cautiously.

152

"She's your daughter, that much is obvious. She's got just as much sass as you and scrutinizes everything I do. Which is odd since I'm the one that should be watching everything."

"It's weird having her here."

"It's an adjustment is all."

"Tell me about it. Usually, by now, I'd be saying goodbye."

"But you're not and that scares you," I say, moving into a sitting position on the bed.

"She, um, was looking at the video game systems today."

"And? What's wrong with that?"

"Nothing, except there aren't any games."

"There are in her room. However, yours are still locked away in my room."

"I was thinking maybe tomorrow, while they're at the doctor, we can run into town."

I run a hand over my chin, studying her closely. "We can, but only on one condition." Angelica lifts a brow at me. "You have to stay beside me at all times and I will put your ass in the car anytime I feel it necessary. You haven't been out of here yet. I'm not sure how you will handle it."

"I think I can handle a toy store and maybe lunch."

"How about Walmart and lunch?"

Angelica looks at me like I have two heads. *"Walmart?"*

"Well, yeah. I need stuff for Tuesday."

"Why? What are we doing Tuesday?"

"It's the fourth and we have company. Plus, Steve is bringing his family, Brent, Marissa, and Ringo."

"And you planned on telling me when?"

"Tomorrow. It's better if I give you as little notice as

possible. You tend to freak out."

Angelica laughs a lot and mutters to herself about freaking out and says something to the effect of she's taking a shower before walking into the bathroom. No sooner than I hear the water turn on, then the bedroom door opens and in walks Angela.

"Angela, aren't you supposed to be in bed?"

"I couldn't sleep. I was hoping I could sleep in here with you guys."

"Um," I pause, "do Janice and Alec let you do that?"

"Sometimes." Angela shrugs.

"Then I suppose. Climb up here and I'm gonna let your mom know."

Angela climbs into bed as I head for the bathroom. I walk in and shut the door behind me. Angelica is working on soaping herself up when I wrap my hand around her mouth, pulling her away from the water and pinning her against the wall with a finger over my mouth. Angelica is watching me, bugged eyed, and her heart is no doubt racing.

"I'm going to move my hand, but you have to be quiet as there's a kid in your bed. Nod your head if you can keep quiet." A smile spreads underneath my hand as she nods her head. I move my hand from her mouth and run a hand through my hair.

"Have you lost your mind? You scared the crap out of me."

"Well, I didn't want you screaming the shrill thing you do. You'd wake up everyone in the house, plus the cat."

"What do you want?"

"I think I need to go to my room tonight."

"No!"

"Yes!" I say sternly. "Think of it this way, you and Angela can have a night together."

"Whatever. Can I finish my shower now?"

"Don't get upset with me. I'm not comfortable with a kid in the bed with me."

"And what if I said you might have to get used to it?"

My eyes go wide then I search my brain for the exact calculations of when her last period was, then her ovulation date, and last but most certainly not least, when we started having sex. She can't be pregnant. I wipe the sweat off my forehead to see that Angelica is wrapped in a towel and sitting on the toilet.

"Angela isn't leaving?"

Angelica shakes her head, "Not if Janice has her way."

I lean up against the sink. "What happened?"

"Alec is sicker than he looks and she can't handle them both."

"Angelica, I'm not good with kids. Hell, I've never even really been around them. She's your daughter, you can't just let her life be hanging in the air till they decide what's going on. Angela needs to be with you and you know it."

Angelica runs her hands through her hair and clears her throat. "I don't know what to do. How's it fair to uproot Angela's life?"

"What's your gut telling you to do?"

"To take her and tell everyone else to suck it."

"Then do just that. Take her and tell everyone to suck it."

"I just wanna get through this week."

I walk over and squat in front of her. "Cupcake, you know delaying won't help anything. That little girl loves you and she needs you to step up and be a mom."

"What about you?"

"What about me?"

"I mean you make it pretty obvious you don't want anything to do with kids."

"It's not that. I can't control kids, nobody can. I lose all control because the kids take it. If you know anything about me, it's that I hate losing control. As for us, we can make it work. I just don't think I should be sleeping in the same bed as her."

"So, Mister Control is saying we take it as it comes?"

"I'm saying you do what you need to do to put your family back together."

Angelica wipes a tear from her face. "You should go if you're going."

I stand and kiss her on the forehead before leaving. I shut the bathroom door as I step out. Looking over at the bed, Angela is laying down and I'm assuming asleep. Only she's not alone. Lucille is laying on top of her. I shake my head, walking over to where I was laying. I intend to grab my book, but it's in Angela's hands.

I sit on the edge of the bed and work on getting it out of her hands. Just as I get it away from her, her eyes pop open. "Go back to sleep. I'm just going down the hall so you and Mommy can sleep together."

"Why? You sleep here too."

"I just figured you'd want some time with Mommy without everyone else."

Angela scrunches her little nose up. "Why?" she asks again while she pats the bed.

I look at the bedroom door, then back to Angela. "Are you sure you don't just want it to be you and

Mommy tonight?"

"No, silly, now come on. I'm sleepy," Angela says to me.

I take a deep breath and get into bed with her. I watch the bathroom door for Angelica, but she must be taking her sweet ass time. While I'm making myself comfortable, Angela snuggles into me. It's weird, but there's an odd feeling at the same time. I wrap an arm around her back and her little head is on my shoulder. Angela is snoring in no time and it makes things a bit more peaceful.

27

ANGELICA

WALMART. The huge beige building looms ahead of us. I can't remember the last time I was in one of these. God, it's been years. I'm not a total snob, it's just that I've had people who did all my shopping for me if I needed it done at all. As I've said, before this last stint in rehab, I was rarely home, now I never leave.

The sun on my face feels good. I'm dressed incognito in Capris, kitten heels, a tank, and cropped cotton jacket. I did full makeup because you never know who's gonna be around. I haven't been seen in months and the band has been handling all our new album's promo since it dropped last month. I haven't even heard the finished product, but I guess that it was good since they produced and put it out on time.

Angela is up ahead of Maverick and me, grabbing a cart and waiting just a bit impatiently as we approach.

"You alright, Cupcake?" he asks me, squeezing my hand.

"Yeah." I smile. "What are we getting for tomorrow?"

"Let me worry about that. Seems you've got a little girl who's looking to shop." He half-laughs as Angela pulls another cart, handing it to me.

I raise an eye at her. "You think you need your own?" I ask with a grin.

"Janice gave me fifty dollars to get some toys." She beams at me.

"She did?"

Angela nods happily, digging into her pocket and pulling out the fifty-dollar bill, which is now a crumpled mess.

I look at Maverick and he just grabs a cart of his own. "We'll start in toys, then electronics, and end in food." He doesn't give me much to argue against. I just nod at him and follow him as he pulls out a list and Angela giggles, moving up beside me.

❖ ❖ ❖

We've gotten a few looks and there have been some whispers. I think I've been spotted a few times, but the people have been good enough to leave us be. In the toy section, Angela hightails it around the corner and I'm left chasing her down as she comes up to the Barbie's and similar dolls. I've been dreading this section, seeing as they merchandised us from the last tour. Us *Fallen Angels* are now dolls for every kid's enjoyment.

"Look, Mommy, they have your doll finally!" She holds up the figure and I hear Maverick chuckle behind me as I groan. It's not a horrible likeness, but my head is a tad too big and the blonde hair is way too blonde. It's platinum while I'm more of a champagne. The makeup is all blues and purples, and it's wearing mile-high wedges, a leather mini with buckles and straps hanging

159

down like something out of a bad S and M movie with a purple and blue corset top, and my signature, a crystal covered silver tutu. What do you want? It's a bit of bling for the stage. The pose has it almost devouring the microphone.

"Thirty-five dollars?" I scoff, seeing that it's the sale price. Hell, do I wanna know how much they are hosing these parents for when it's not on sale?

"I have everyone else, just not you," she says, putting it in her cart which also has some snacks in it for later. Kettle corn, roasted sunflower seeds, trail mix with the M&M's, and dark chocolate covered Acai berries, the kid has healthier eating habits than I do *without* being told.

I just smile as she grabs a second one and hands it to me. "You should have one too." She is all smiles, seems she is proud of her momma. I take the doll and put it in my otherwise still empty cart. I don't know why I even took one at this point. Everything is going smoothly until we hit electronics and I see *it*.

There it is, right on the endcap, a life-size, standing cardboard cutout of Brent and me, *singing*. My heart skips a beat. I remember that photo shoot, it was just before we left for Sydney. I was so coked up I couldn't see straight and what should have been an hour shoot took like three. They had to pack on a pound of makeup to cover the circles under my eyes from the bender I had been on all weekend with Kyle.

"Mommy! Look, it's you and Brent!" Angela squeals and several people turn, looking at us. The cat out of the bag, they come up to me, wanting autographs *and* pictures. I freeze, but only for a moment since Angela is watching with the proudest little look on her beautiful face. Maverick takes a step toward me and I put out my hand to stay him. I can do this. *I have to be able to do this.* The small crowd starts snapping pics with their cell phones as I'm handed a Sharpie and all manner of things to sign. The department manager, Heather, comes out and insists that I take a picture with her. I smile graciously and pose. I don't know how many of these are gonna wind up on Facebook and Instagram, but I'm betting that the social media is gonna go nuts in the next thirty minutes or so.

The manager is helpful, making sure Angela gets the games she wants, but I'm getting twitchy and Maverick must be seeing it because the next thing I know, he's apologizing and pulling me from the throngs of people. He quickly has me under the arm, directing Angela and me away.

"Thank you," I whisper, leaning over and kissing him on the cheek softly.

He just smiles as we turn into the clothing section, following Angela, who's taken off ahead yet again.

* * *

Maverick's cart is full of fresh fruits and veggies as well as steaks and since Angela requested it, shrimp, lobster, and pork steaks. We couldn't find any crawdads, but I promised Angela we would go to the fish market on the other side of town later in the week and pick some up. She's happy with that compromise.

By the time we get through check out, there are a ton of people outside, all with cell phones up and at the ready. Maverick has to grab Angela and me and shield us from them as we head for the car. This. This is why I had bodyguards. It's why I sent people out. Just shopping can be an ordeal. This sucks, he's never gonna let us out of the house again. He gets us and our bags into the car and starts it up. I look over at him and shake my head. "Welcome to dating a rockstar. So, how's about that lunch?"

He white knuckles the steering wheel as we pull out of the parking lot. "How's about we go home and I make you lunch? Or we stop for Chinese along the way?"

I sigh. "I'm sorry, I should have warned you that this might happen, what with *Lucid Dreams* dropping while we've been going through the motions at home."

"It's nothing to worry about, just forget it," he says softly, looking in the rearview mirror at Angela, who's rifling through her bag and chomping down on some sunflower seeds.

❊ ❊ ❊

The house is thankfully quiet. Janice and Alec aren't back yet. Maverick heads for the kitchen with the foodstuffs, so I take Angela and all her new things to her room. She picked up some cute little summer dresses, a new boy short tankini with Tinkerbell on it and we got matching white mules because I can't say no to new shoes. She also needed some bras. I noticed that the trainer she's wearing isn't cutting it, turns out the kid is already wearing a thirty-two B. My goodness, she's only nine! The games she bought are of the multiplayer variety, the *Hasbro Family Pack* with Monopoly and Risk as well as *Just Dance 2 Disney Edition*. She also got *Lollipop Chainsaw* for my 360 and a racing game that she thinks she's gonna talk Maverick into playing. I don't know about that, but I'll certainly play the *Just Dance* one with her.

We grabbed Chinese on the way home, but Maverick hasn't eaten yet. He took off for the bedroom soon after we got home, leaving Angela and me alone. I take to hooking up the Xbox One in the living room where the fifty-five-inch TV is and she and I play a few rounds of her game. She's handing me my ass for the second time when Janice and Alec come in.

"Hey," I shout over the blasting television, grabbing the control and pausing it. Angela bemoans and stops dancing, watching us.

"Hi," Janice says as Alec heads for the kitchen and gets himself a bottle of water from the fridge.

"How'd it go?" I ask, my eyes darting back and forth between them.

Janice shakes her head and walks over to Alec, putting a hand on his shoulder. "Not how we had hoped. The PET scan shows that it's moved into his bones."

"I-I'm sorry."

"Have you given any thought to what you and Janice talked about?" Alec asks, looking over at Angela, his eyes glazing.

"I have." I nod. "I'll do whatever you think is best."

"We have the papers. You may want your lawyer to look them over after the holiday, but really all you need to do is sign them and have a witness, then file with the clerk's office," Janice adds as Alec heads for the bedroom. He looks like a broken man and who can blame him. If the cancer is in the bones, a year is a gift.

28

MAVERICK

WALMART WAS A NIGHTMARE. I was on edge from the time we walked through the door and people started watching every step we took. Angela kept running off and it drove me nuts. Then she screamed out and I was ready to pick them both up and walk out. I know it's the life of a rockstar, but this said Rockstar is still in the beginning stages of her rehab. Angelica still has a long road ahead of her and now it seems she may be doing it with a kid in tow.

I picked up the Chinese I ordered on the way back to the house. Angelica and Angela are in the kitchen eating now. I've headed off to the bedroom because I need a few minutes alone to gather my thoughts. I've barely stepped into my room and Angelica's phone is on my desk going crazy. Three long strides and I'm at my desk, picking up the phone. Scrolling through it, I see we are all over fucking social media. Thankfully, *mystery man* doesn't have social media, so they are having a hard time figuring me out. I've done well to keep myself cut off from all the social media bullshit. However, now I'm

Angelica's mystery man.

I pull my phone out of my pocket as it starts ringing. I don't even check who's calling before growling into the phone, "What?"

I hear Steve laughing on the other end of the line. "Welcome to the tabloids."

I'm not in the mood to chit chat, so I cut to the point, "What do you need, *Steve*?"

"I was checking to make sure you were okay. You know, see if you've seen it yet."

"I've seen it and I'm fine."

"Does *she* know?"

"No. I just got them home and now they are eating."

"Well, she posed for the pictures, so I'm sure she kind of expected. God, what was she thinking."

"I didn't pose for shit, but they have one of her kissing me. Fucking bullshit. As for her thoughts, her fucking daughter was eating it all up and she wanted to impress her."

"Do you want me to call everyone and cancel tomorrow?"

"No, everyone just needs to be on their best behavior. I'm already gonna have my hands full with Angelica and Angela. Plus, they both already know. We can't cancel everything now."

"Alright, so what time do you want us there?"

"At this point, you could show up tonight and I wouldn't care," I say just as I snap Angelica's phone in my hand. "FUCK!"

"What was that? Are you alright?"

"I broke Angelica's phone. The fucking thing won't quit going off and now there are pictures of the kid everywhere. Son of a bitch!" I drop the phone and examine my hand. "Steve, I've got to go give myself a few stitches."

"Alright, man, we'll be there around eleven so we can start cooking. We can just chill and eat all day. That's how we do it at my house. Sound good to you?"

"Yeah, that works. See you then."

Dropping my phone on the desk, I head straight for the bathroom. Blood's fucking everywhere. I go about cleaning my left hand before getting my thread and needle ready. I'm about halfway through when I hear 'Ouch' come from Angelica's mouth. My head shoots up to look at her and I can tell from the look on her face that she knows I'm pissed. She doesn't dare speak another word and for her sake, it's a good fucking thing. She points toward the bedroom which, I'm going to assume, means she's waiting in there. So be it.

I finish with my hand, so I clean up the bathroom before walking into the bedroom where I find Angelica sitting on my bed.

"Angelica, what the fuck did you think you were doing today?"

Angelica clears her throat, "I was doing what the guys do all the time and I never usually get to do."

"Guess what? You aren't one of the guys. I tried to stop it and you put your hand up at me. Have you lost your ever-loving mind?" I am breathing hard, but trying to keep my voice down.

"Maverick, you don't understand, I'm the face of that band. That was me on the cardboard. Once I was spotted what did you expect me to do?"

"I do understand. I know it was, Angelica. I'm not fucking stupid like you seem to think I am. As for what did I expect? I expected you let me do my fucking job, but no, you put your hand up like I'm some fucking dog.

News flash, Cupcake, I don't bow down and I won't be made a fool of either."

Angelica stands up and is damn near up against me. "I wasn't trying to do any of that to you. These are the things that are expected of me. Signing autographs, taking pictures and dealing with fans. All of the stuff I avoided when I was high and that Christy used to get on to me for never doing."

"Angelica, not only is it you all over social media, it's Angela and me as well. There's a picture of you fucking kissing me. I'm now your mystery man."

Angelica sighs, putting her hand over her eyes. "Christ."

"What kind of phone do you want? I need to order you a new one," I try asking her a simple question as I take a seat at my desk.

"Doesn't really matter since I don't have access to it anyhow. So, don't worry about it."

"Fine!" I snap, pushing the food Angelica must have brought in here away. "What did you need when you came in here?"

"To bring you some food and make sure you were okay. It'd been a while since I'd seen you."

"I'm peachy. Stitches in my hand. All over social media. Yup, just fucking peachy."

Angelica walks up behind me, wrapping her arms around my neck. "Please, calm down," she whispers, then kiss me behind the ear. "It's not like it's a sex tape. You should have seen Brent and Marissa's video."

I stand, grabbing her, pushing her to the bed and straddling her in a flash. "This isn't fucking funny. Angelica, I had zero and I do mean zero, fucking social media presence. I've been able to stay away from the bullshit it brings."

"Maverick, stop, you're hurting me!"

I loosen my grip, but watch her expectantly.

Angelica moves under me, but I don't budge. "Angelica, stop. You must see that this whole day could have been stopped with one fucking sentence. Why couldn't you just let me do my job? I'm still your bodyguard."

"Get the fuck off me, Maverick!" Angelica shouts at me.

"Fine. What the fuck ever. Do what you want. Apparently, nothing from this past month has sunk in. I'm done!" I shout, pushing myself off her before grabbing my phone and slamming the door on the way out.

I head straight for the front door. Once I'm out the door, I just start walking. I don't think about where I'm going, just walking.

* * *

I've been outside for hours now. I've walked all over the property. Now I'm sitting out by the pool and all the lights in the house are out. I fucking cracked and it's killing me. I've never laid a hand on a woman in anger in my life. I just don't get how she was cracking jokes. This shit isn't funny. Christ's sakes, Angelica has made me cry more than anyone. I can't even face her because of what I did.

My head is in my hands when I hear Steve's voice behind me. "You calmed the fuck down yet?"

I jerk my head up, wiping the tears from my face before looking at Steve. "I'm working on it. What are you doing here?"

"Angelica called me."

"I figured that was coming. You here to watch me pack my shit?"

Steve gives me a half-cocked grin and shakes his head. "No, man, it's not like you strangled her."

"I shouldn't have fucking touched her. I don't know what the fuck happened. I've never done anything like that."

"Yeah, well, you scared her."

"I scared *me*."

"She's not an easy woman to love."

"I never said I love her."

"Dude, it's all over your face, so don't give me that shit."

"Guilt is all over my face, not love. I can't love someone and do what I did to her. That isn't love."

"It can be both. Do you realize you've done the one thing none of us could do?"

"Scare her?"

"Got her to love you back."

"She doesn't need to love me. She deserves someone better than me."

Steve shakes his head again, walking over to me and placing his bear paw of a hand on my shoulder. "You weren't ready for what happened today. It's not easy getting splashed all over the papers, because that's what's coming, be sure of it."

"I could have stopped it all, had she not put that fucking hand in my face. I was ready to drag her out by her hair after that. I gave her rules and she fucking ignored them."

"She thought it was something she *needed* to do. She was wrong."

"Yeah, I tried to tell her that, but she would rather crack jokes about fucking sex tapes than be serious."

"She brought up Brent and Marissa…"

"Yes, but honestly, at this point, I couldn't care less. I've been pissed. I've wanted to snap her fucking neck. She made me crack wide open and now I've cried like a fucking fool because of everything that's gone down. Not much more I can do besides pack my shit and move on."

"That's the last thing anybody wants, man. Especially her."

"I can't keep doing this. I do the shit I do because she was getting better because of it. In one fucking day, she's lost all the work we did."

"I'd say you're right, but she doesn't have a pill in her mouth or bottle in her hand. All she's doing is crying."

"That's because I cleared out the whole house before she came home. There's nothing but stuff that is good for her in that house. So, she couldn't get it."

Steve laughs. "She called *me* instead of her *dealer*. That has to count for something."

I rub my left hand over my face and pull it away quickly, shaking it out. It fucking stings. "I don't know. I'm glad she called you, but she shouldn't have had to. I should have just stayed the fuck away from her."

"Are you talking about today or in general?"

"All of it. I should have never even thought of her that way. When she kissed me, I should have backed off and kept it that way."

Steve chuckles. "Yeah? Well, you did, and now you're in deep. You're going to fight. Question is… Is she worth it? To you?"

A stray tear falls down my face. "Every fucking second. I get a different side than most people see of her. I get the *real* her."

"Then what the fuck are we doing out here?"

Steve lifts me out of the seat. "Bleeding to death."

Steve chuckles. "Come inside, Kelly's got sutures and a tetanus shot for you. Then you can go see your girl."

"I don't think that's such a good idea. I think we both need the night."

Steve looks at me. "Do you know why Kellie and I are still married?"

"Because you love each other?"

"That aside. Because we communicate and we make it a habit of not going to bed angry."

29

ANGELICA

MARY ANN AND SUE ELLEN, STEVE'S daughters, are bunking with Angela, for the night. She's glad to have a couple of playmates her own age. I set Kellie and Steve up in one of the other guest rooms as soon as they got here and now I'm in my room with the TV going but not really watching it. Maverick was just *so…* Seeing him angry, it scared me. To think that I was the cause of such rage in him, rage that I couldn't stop. Who did I think I was, some Messiah, as if I could just lay my hands on him and it could still him? I'm not Marissa, and he's certainly not Brent. We don't have that kind of a connection. I don't calm his world down, I set it ablaze.

Maybe he's going to leave, maybe it would be better for him to do that. It would rip my heart out, but he would be better off without me, at least then his world would make sense again. He's not ready to take on all my shit and it's unfair of me to ask him to. With Angela here now, it's even worse. He doesn't want kids, and to push one that doesn't belong to him on to him is wrong on so many levels.

I look up from my stupor to see Maverick standing in the open doorway. I have no idea how long he's been standing there, just watching me. He's changed his clothes and has a proper bandage on his hand. Kellie took care of him, just like she said she would. His eyes are puffy behind his glasses, seems we've both been crying tonight. I swallow hard and I know that he's got something to say, but I'm not sure if I want to hear it. Reaching into my night stand, I get up from the bed and walk over to him. He stiffens on my approach, so I stop a breath away from him and he looks to the floor with something like shame on his face.

I reach up, taking him by the back of the head.

"Angelica, I'm-" he starts and I pull him down to kiss me, pressing the condom into his right hand. He breaks our kiss and I watch as it registers in is head what I've given him. He looks at me, confused.

"I don't need words, just actions," I whisper softly, pulling him into the room and closing the door behind us. He wraps his good hand into the back of my head, pulling it back as his lips find mine once more. I pull him back to the bed and sit, and he pulls my tank off, exposing my heaving chest to the cool night air, my nipples instantly erect. Kneeling down, he takes one into his mouth, devouring it, sucking and biting lightly as he pushes me back toward the center of the bed, climbing on top of me. I pull his shirt off, tossing it over my head so I can run my nails down between his shoulder blades, pulling a moan from him. He kisses down my length, working my shorts off to find I don't wear any panties underneath.

"Nice," he observes with a smile, putting my legs up over his shoulders and burying his face deep in my pussy. I let out a whimper as his tongue delves into me, my shoulders lifting off the bed as he penetrates me over and over again, not stopping until sweat drips from my thighs and I'm clenching the covers in orgasmic bliss. Setting me down, he pulls away from me and I watch with shaking legs as he takes off his pants and puts on the condom before getting back on the bed. Sitting up on his knees, he reaches for me, so I take his forearm and he lifts me to his chest.

"Ride my cock," he demands, fisting the thing in his hand, holding it steady for me to settle down on. I pop up on my knees, having to nearly stand on the bed to take it into me and gasp as the thick head passes over my ridge and I take him inside me completely. "Thatta girl." He grabs my ass with his good hand and makes me pick up the pace. It takes a minute, but we find our rhythm. Fuck, he feels good inside me. My body opens up to him, responds to his mouthy assaults on my tits, my neck, my mouth, and I am coming again fast and hard. I tense up around his stiff veined cock as it plunders my body for every drop of cum it can manage. I'm leaning against him, trying to catch my breath, but he's not finished with me. Pulling out of me, he lays me down to feast on my flesh again before fucking me with hard abandon once more.

The comforter is drenched in sweat and God knows what else when we finally find ourselves lying there with heaving chests. I'm still on top of him with his cock inside me, finally going soft. I kiss him tenderly, sliding off him, and he heads for the bathroom to get rid of the condom. By the time he comes back, I have already stripped the comforter from the bed and am lying under the sheet. He climbs back into the bed with me and I curl up into his arms. I'm exhausted, and all I really want to do now is sleep in his arms.

* * *

I wake to the rising sun and apparently, a very horny Maverick.

"Roll over, I need to be balls deep in you right now," he growls into my ear.

"I need to get up, there's a houseful that's gonna be hungry," I say, laughing as I'm pulled onto my back with kisses to my neck. "Hmm…" His hand is between my thighs and his hard cock is already pressing against me.

"Don't make me tell you twice." His tone is commanding and I reach into the nightstand for a condom. I've barely got it on him and he's on me, pushing slowly, each thrust more maddening than the last as he rubs my clit with his thumb, his head buried in my shoulder. I wrap my legs around his hips, locking him against me as he gets faster, harder, bouncing me off the bed as I quake against him. It doesn't last long, but it's enough to make me ache in all the right places.

With legs of jelly, I lay there as he pants softly in my ear. "Sleeping in here has perks."

I let out a laugh. "Ya think?" I shimmy out from under him. "I'm gonna go grab a shower and start breakfast. See ya out there in a bit?"

"You got it, Cupcake." He smiles, watching me head through the bathroom door.

Showered and dressed for the day, I head out to the kitchen to find Kellie pulling out food. "What are you up to?" I ask as she turns toward me.

"Hey, you okay?" she asks, eyeing me cautiously.

"Yeah," I answer, running my hand through my

hair. "We've moved passed it... I think." I end with a nervous chuckle.

"Fucked your way passed it, did ya?" She grins as I look at her with reddening cheeks. "Sorry, couldn't help but hear ya as I was passing by this morning."

"Sorry."

"No need to be, sweets. It's your house, do as you please."

"Thanks. So, you want some help there?" I ask, watching as she sets out my waffle mix, syrup, bacon, and potatoes.

"Nope, I got it. Least I can do for you putting us up last night."

"Nonsense, you fixed Maverick up, was the least I could do."

"Let's call it even and I'll do breakfast since you all will be cooking come lunch and dinner. Crystal will be here with Ringo, and Brent and Marissa in a few hours, so you'll need to be on your toes for that."

"Right." I haven't seen them since Aspen, after the Ecstasy spike at the club in Los Angeles that sent Brent into a tailspin. That was just before my overdose. Sheesh, has it already been three months?

She looks around. "Don't you have a coffee pot?"

"Um, I think Maverick put it up. He says I'm not allowed to have any kind of stimulants," I answer sheepishly and she raises an eye at me.

"Maverick says?" She purses her lips. "And I thought my Dom was hard on me.

"He's not my *Dom*," I deadpan as she goes through my cabinets.

"He tells you what to do, in and out of the bedroom, what to eat, what chores need to be done, when and how you should sleep, and when you're good, you get rewards. Honey, that's practically a 24/7 D/s relationship's definition. All he needs to be doing now is smacking that ass on the regular and for you to like it."

I think back to this morning, he may not have hit me, but he pounded me good and hard and with a very commanding tone. Christ, am I in a fetish relationship? The look on my face must have been classic because Kellie looks at me and laughs.

"Oh, honey, ain't nothing to be ashamed of, if it works for ya, it works for ya. But me, I need coffee… Ah ha!" She pulls out my twelve-pot coffee maker.

"Good luck, I don't have any coffee in the house."

"Oh, Steve packed us good. I got coffee. I'm a snob about it and only drink fresh ground, I even bring my own grinder."

I shake my head as she shows me the grinder and pound of coffee beans already waiting on the counter. "Well, you enjoy that, I'll have my juice."

"Suit yourself."

About half way through Kellie cooking, the girls get up. Angela is the first to appear and Steve's girls aren't far behind her.

"Morning, Mommy." Angela kisses me and I pour her and the other two some milk. We're gonna need more soon, especially if everyone else takes it with their coffee. Janice and Alec, who've been scarce, emerge and help themselves to some. I introduce them to Kellie and Steve when he comes out in basketball shorts and no shirt. He's covered in tattoos, like all the men in my life, and it looks like he's gone back to the gym recently as he's shredded.

"Good to finally meet you," Steve says, shaking Alec's hand. "You've done a mighty fine job with the little Hellcat." He smiles, looking at Angela who sticks her tongue out at him. The pair is fully dressed and refuse breakfast. Instead, Janice informs me that they are flying out this afternoon.

I take her aside. "What do you mean you're leaving today?" I ask, watching from the patio as Angela and the girls set up the video game in the living room while the food is cooking.

"We think it's best. We already changed the flight and a car will be here in about an hour to get us. Alec will give you the papers for the lawyer before we go."

"What am I supposed to tell Angela? I mean you're going and she isn't."

"She *knows*." Alec joins us outside. "We told her that this was not just a visit for her, that you were planning on keeping her, finally."

"You- I mean- what do you mean she knows? And she's just okay?"

"I think she's just happy to see you. It's going to be an adjustment, but in the long run, worth it for you both," Janice answers my flabbergasted questions.

"You don't think just skipping out isn't going to affect her? What about all her stuff, her school, friends, did she even get to say goodbye?"

"You'll either enroll her in something here in the fall or home school. Perhaps, whatever Steve does for those two. As for her stuff, we will make arrangements to have it all shipped to you by next week, it's already packed, and friends, well, she was acting up, so it's better she start fresh here and it appears she's already doing that." Alec puts a hand on my shoulder and I shy away.

"You-you just assumed I would go along with all of this? What if I'd not been as good as I am? What if I was still fucked up, then what would you have done?"

They look at each other, then back to me. "We'd have talked to your mom," Alec says. "That was our final option."

"What? How the fuck could you? She's still with that monster. Do you think he'd keep off her just because she's his? It wouldn't have mattered." I haul off and smack him and I'm instantly grabbed. I turn around to find Maverick pulling me into his chest as I claw my way toward them.

"I think you've overstayed your welcome," he states matter-of-factly. Janice and Alec nod and scoot passed me as I snarl, clinging to Maverick. "Hey, easy, they're going, that's all that matters."

"My mother!" I whisper, grinding my teeth down. "If I'd been unfit, they would have sent my baby to her. I'd have killed them, seriously, killed them."

He cradles my head, rubbing down my hair. "Shh, Cupcake, it's okay, you're okay, and Angela is gonna be just fine now that she's here with us."

30

MAVERICK

JANICE AND ALEC HAVE LEFT AND *without* Angela. I suppose Angelica and I will be talking about homeschooling. For now, I just need to get us through the day unscathed. I'm trying to keep myself calm and collected, all while letting Angelica know I'm beside her.

Walking into the kitchen, I spot the coffee pot. *What the hell?* Everyone is in here because Kellie made breakfast. I glance at Angelica, waiting for some form of explanation.

"Coffee?" I ask and wait for someone to answer.

"Oh, I don't go anywhere without it. Don't worry, your little pet had her juice," Kellie says, oh so matter of factly.

I clench my jaw and look to Steve, who's fucking laughing. I turn my eyes back to Kellie. "That's not good for you. If you need it, I'm sure your husband would be more than happy to help you with your little problem."

Kellie looks at me for a moment before taking a drink of her coffee. "Mmm, so good," she moans.

I nod before grabbing water and an apple from the

fridge and walking from the room without another word.

I'm sitting at my desk, watching the cameras when my door opens and closes behind me. I don't have to turn around to know who it is. I saw her coming. A fruit bowl with yogurt and granola is slid on the table in front of me.

"Thank you, but I'd have been okay with the apple for today."

"I'm sorry about that, she took over my kitchen."

"It's not your fault, Cupcake."

"I should've been a little more assertive."

"No, they should have had the courtesy to not have shit here that I'm keeping out of your diet. But it's already blown to hell with breakfast. "

"Let's face it, it was going to be blown to hell with lunch and dinner too."

"Not with me cooking, it won't be. They will just have to deal."

"Yeah, but I plan to stuff myself like a turkey." Angelica giggles.

I turn the chair so I can look at her. Pulling her into my lap, I ask, "And if I don't want you to?"

Angelica looks at me as if she's taken aback by what I asked. "Then I guess I'm a naughty little sub because I want to eat."

I watch her for a second, confused. Then what Kellie said in the kitchen catches in my head. She called Angelica my pet and Angelica is calling herself a sub. "Sub? Pet? What the hell are you on about, woman?"

"Kellie has it in her head that you and I are in a twenty-four seven D and S relationship."

Again, I watch her, confused. I turn back to the computer, never moving Angelica from my lap. I pull up the browser and begin typing. D and S are Dominant and Submissive. We don't have that kind of thing going on. *Do we?* I look at Angelica for a brief second, then back to the computer in front of me. I have control, yes, but does that really make me a dominant?

"Angelica, this isn't us. I don't beat you. I sure as hell don't have some red fucking room."

Angelica looks at me and just laughs. "I don't think you have to smack me around for it to be what it is."

I shake my head and wipe my mouth with my left hand and the sting hits me. "Shit," I hiss before looking into Angelica's eyes. "I'm not dominant," I grit out.

"You might not think so, but it makes sense and it gets worse the more flustered you get. The thing is, I like it."

"You like that I'm *controlling*? But last night, I hurt you. I saw the bruise on your shoulder this morning."

"That was different. I like what you do when you're not angry."

I hang my head in disgust. "What if I can't stop it and it happens again?" I ask, not looking back at her.

Angelica runs her hands through my hair. "We work on *my* sobriety and *your* anger management."

"You know, I never had a problem with my anger before you, strutting around naked and bucking against me at every turn."

"I will try to frustrate you less, but you know there are still a lot of rooms in this house we haven't christened."

"Yeah, well, we have a house full. One of them is your nine-year-old. I think it's time to get you off my lap and back to everyone else before my cock gets any harder."

Angelica smiles. "While I've noticed that. I'm still

not walking straight from this morning. So, I'm going to have to pass."

Angelica kisses me sloppily and tries lifting herself off me. I pull her back down to my cock tightening in my shorts. I rock myself against her aching core. The little moan she lets out tells me she wants me. I run my hands up her legs slowly as I nip at her bottom lip. Her creamy skin smells of orchids, it's the same smell that makes me forget what I'm doing.

Angelica melts into me as I nip and lick my way to her neck. "We are going to do this and you need to keep quiet. No loud noises. Too many witnesses. Understand?" Angelica breathlessly manages an *'uh huh'* before I go back to exploring every inch of her body. Gripping her ass in my hands, I stand and walk us both to the bathroom.

Sitting her down on the sink, I begin removing her shirt and bra. I go from sucking her pert little nipples to nibbling and placing small kisses on her chest, stomach, and sides as I make my way to her shorts. Her moans start getting louder as I stand her up and begin helping her out of her shorts and panties. My girl is freshly waxed and my cock twitches in my pants. I swipe a finger through her folds and she's already wet and wanting.

"Jesus, you smell amazing," I say, sucking the finger in my mouth with her on it. "And you taste even better," I groan.

Using my middle finger, I find her core and bring her almost to the brink before pulling out. I bring it to her mouth and she opens and sucks it all the way in before licking around it, then lets it go with a pop.

I lick my lips and watch Angelica closely. I'm about to take her for the ride of her life. Burying my face in her pussy, I lick and suck, all while pressing against and playing with her clit. Her knees are shaking and she's having trouble staying up on her own. I place her legs over my shoulders before looking at her. "You might want to hold on for this," I smirk then dive back in.

Finally, after I've had my fill of her with my mouth and let her come, not once, but three times, I place her back on the sink as I reach in and turn the shower on before stripping my clothes. My cock is bobbing between us and she hums approvingly. After checking the water to make sure it's good, I lift her up, wrapping her legs around my waist.

"I love you, Cupcake. Now hold on to me and remember, *keep quiet*." I smile before thrusting into her at the same time as I crash my mouth to hers.

Angelica matches me thrust for thrust. She feels fucking amazing wrapped around my throbbing cock. I groan into her shoulder and I fuck her into the wall over and over. I press a hand over her mouth when she screams out as she's coming.

I can feel her tightening around my cock and I know the pressure in her is already building up again. I can feel my own release beginning as my sack tightens. I bring a thumb to Angelica's clit and she's begging me to bring her over the edge. I barely put pressure on her clit and she shatters.

"One more, Cupcake, just give me one more. You feel so fucking good wrapped around me."

Angelica bites down on my shoulder and I'm about to explode. With my thumb on her clit and my cock bringing her over another edge, I am grunting and trying not to scream out.

"Fuck. Yes. Cupcake." Angelica's little hand palms my sack and I piston in her harder and deeper with every thrust.

"Maverick, I'm coming," Angelica hisses before kissing me hard. That's all it takes and we're coming together. Pressing my forehead to hers, we're both breathing hard and holding onto one another for dear life.

❖ ❖ ❖

Once Angelica and I clean ourselves up and get dressed, we walk out to the living room with my arm around her shoulders and one of hers around my waist. I look down at her. "Ready for this?" I ask.

Angelica shakes her head no. "I can do this," she says with zero confidence.

I turn toward her and place my hand on her cheek. "I'm right beside you, Cupcake. Or do I need to show you that again?"

A smile spreads across her face at my comment. "*Later*. I'm hungry."

"Then I suppose I should feed ya, huh?" I take Angelica's hand in mine and we walk out the patio doors to find everyone else has shown up. I glance around. I smile at Angelica then kiss her on the forehead. "I'm going to see if Steve needs any help. Go sit with the ladies while I figure out lunch."

I walk away, leaving Angelica to sit with the girls. I'll keep my eye on her, plus I have my tablet in my back pocket so I can watch her if she goes inside. It's the only foolproof way to make sure she doesn't need me. Ringo and Steve are on the grill as I make my way to them.

"Food smells good."

Steve looks at me. "Yeah, I'm sure you worked up an appetite."

"Steve's good on the grill. Better us than Brent or we'd never eat today." Ringo chuckles.

"Nice to see you again, Ringo. All goes well, I hope." I completely ignore Steve's comment as I watch Ringo.

"Same shit, different day. How's *our* girl doing?" Ringo asks, watching Angelica.

The way he watches her tells me he's fucked her at some point. I'll stay calm, it was before my time. So that's two because I'm positive Steve has as well. "She's doing good, only a few hiccups since she's been home, but we've found ways to work through them," I answer him then turn back to Steve. I'm not going to get into a battle of wits with an unarmed person. "Is anything done? Angelica is hungry."

"Shrimp's up, chops are just about done, some of the ribs are done, and we got burgers on top," Steve says.

"Cupcake?" I yell for Angelica and she looks at me. "Come get you some food."

Angelica jumps up and walks over to me. The girls at the table are snickering. The girls in the pool are giggling like hyenas and this is the first-time Brent's looked at me. Now, it's almost like he's sizing me up. I'm broken out of my thoughts by a hand on my face.

"What's rattling around in that head of yours?" Angelica asks as I look down at her.

"All good, Cupcake."

Angelica pats me on the chest. "*Okay.*"

My phone rings and I let her know I'll be back. Pulling the phone from my pocket, I head inside.

"Hello?" I say without looking at who is calling.

"*Mister Donovan.*" I hear Christy say sarcastically.

"How are you, Mister Christy?"

"Do you have something to tell me?"

I pull the tablet out of my back pocket and get it set up so I can watch Angelica while I deal with this phone call. "She's doing good. Got company here right now. She went out yesterday and for the most part, she did okay."

"Are we leaving out the part that you're fucking her on my dime."

"To be technical, she's paying me. Not you."

"Well, let's see if she continues to pay you on time because Imogen is no longer employing you."

"Got it. Thank you for your call."

We hang up and I drop my phone on the counter beside the tablet. I knew this day was coming. I'll have to break the news to Angelica tonight. I know it won't go over well, but I can't stay here if I'm not working. I have to make a living.

Watching the tablet, I see that all the girls are down by the pool and the guys are on the patio by the grill. Just as I'm about to head back out, I hear someone burst through the front door. I walk that way and come face to face with who can only be Kyle Casey because Brent's outside.

"Hey, Queenie, where you at? Let's get this party started."

"How can I help you, *Kyle*?" I ask, stopping in front of him.

"You can start by getting the fuck out of my way. I'm not here for you."

Kyle reeks of booze. "You weren't invited and you are definitely not staying in your shape. I'd suggest you leave."

"Yeah, funny thing about invitations getting lost, huh? Can't invite one brother and not the other.

187

ANGELICA!"

"If I'm correct, I did just that. Because he is, well, sober and you aren't."

"Who the fuck do you think you are? You aren't anything but the help. Flavor of the week. Give me ten minutes and she'll be back on her knees for me, like always."

I don't say another word. Instead, I swing and my fist connects with his nose. He goes down, blood spewing everywhere. I'm already fired, why not have a little fun.

Kyle's up and rushing me in no time. "Son of a bitch."

I block his tackle, the advantage of being sober, and he goes back down, head smacking the coffee table. "I may be the son of a bitch, but that's life. You had enough yet?"

Kyle spits blood. "I ain't even got started."

"Then we do this like men and you quit trying to tackle like a pussy. You got fists, use them, or do you not know how?"

Kyle's ready, fighting stance and all. "Bitch, you ain't got a clue."

Kyle begins throwing punches. I block one and then he connects with my ribs. I throw one just as he connects with the side of my face. My glasses are gone. Fucker. I'm done playing, time to end this bullshit. I swing and land one on the right side of his face.

"Who do you think you are, putting your hands on *Angelica*?" Kyle grits out.

"The one sleeping in her bed."

Kyle swings again and I block him. "She's ours, you don't have that right."

"You're just jealous because you don't have

someone to stay fucked up with anymore." I swing again and get him right down the middle. If his nose wasn't already broken, it is now.

Next thing I know, I'm being shoved and Kyle's being grabbed by Steve. I throw my hands in the air. "I'm good."

"What the fuck, man? Kyle, what are you doing here?"

"He was talking about Cupcake," I state. Kyle lunges forward and Steve just pulls him back and makes him sit down. "I'm going to get my tablet, I'm done with this bullshit."

I'm just getting to the tablet when Brent, a very pregnant Marissa, and Angelica come into the house. I turn so I can see them. They are all blurry, but I can make them out. Angelica runs straight to me while Brent heads for Kyle.

"Your hand, you're bleeding."

"I'm okay, Cupcake."

"The fuck you are. Kellie!" Angelica screams, dragging me to the sink.

"Really, I'm fine. Can't see worth a damn, but I'm okay."

Angelica grabs me by the head. "I don't even want to know why. I'm just glad you're all right." Then she kisses me.

We break apart as I hear who I'm assuming is Brent shouting. I move Angelica behind me and step out so I can see him better.

"Boy, before you come at me like you're gonna whoop my ass, your brother had it coming. You don't tell me you're gonna have my girl on her knees and wanting you in ten minutes. And while I'm at it, Kyle, as you see, she came to me as you sit there like the pussy you are. I told you to leave as soon as I smelled the fucking booze. She's clean and you aren't fucking changing that. Now, Brent, do we have problems?" I straighten up to my full height, all while watching everything around. It's all blurry but I'm watching and trying to keep Angelica behind me.

Steve smacks Kyle in the back of his head. Brent takes a step toward me and then Marissa steps in front of him. "Oh, I don't think so. You had it coming," she says, pointing at Kyle. "And you would die. I'm not raising these babies by myself," she tells Brent with a finger in his chest.

I feel Angelica's hand rubbing on my back. I look at Steve. "I'm sorry for doing this with your kids here. I told him to leave, but he had to show up just as fucking Christy fired me." Angelica's hand stops moving.

"Hell, I'll hire you. What do you do besides her?"

"We can talk about it later. We need to clean this shit up so we can bring the kids in." I let out a short laugh and pull Angelica around me. "Cupcake, we'll figure it out. We knew this day would come." I place my hand on her face and watch her as closely as I can. "I need to ask you a favor before we talk though."

"Okay?"

"I have spare glasses on my desk. Grab a pair?"

Angelica walks off just as Kellie walks through the door. She mumbles something to Kellie, then I can't hear much else. My adrenaline is coming back down. All the pain is setting in as I get to the chair and sit down.

"You know I meant what I said yesterday," I hear Steve as he comes into the kitchen.

"Forgive me if I have no idea what the fuck you are talking about."

"Regardless of what the idiot said, she loves *you*."

"Yeah, I know, but it just wasn't the time, man. Fucking Christy. I mean I knew it was coming, but I had just hung up when Kyle busted through the front door."

"If anything, the boy has impeccable timing."

"I'm about positive he cracked a few ribs."

"Ah, don't worry about it, Kellie can fix you up."

"Yeah, I'm sure she can. Do me a favor, grab my tablet and see where my glasses are."

31

ANGELICA

KYLE CASEY. Brent's twin brother and my one time fun time guy. His showing up this afternoon was not ideal, in fact, it was downright humiliating. Airing our business to Maverick, I suppose I'm going to have to answer for it eventually. The fact that I've slept with every member of this band at one point or another over the last three years, be it one time or several, doesn't matter, it happened, it's a part of my past. A past that Maverick is going to have to come to terms with. One I need to forgive myself for. Something far more easily said than done.

Kellie fixed my boys up and Kyle is sleeping off his drunk in a guest room. I just couldn't put him out, I couldn't let him drive in his current condition. How he managed to slip his bodyguard, Carlos, and get here in one piece is still beyond my comprehension. Kellie might not be a doctor, but years of working in Triage and trauma centers has lent her considerable experience and she was able to get Maverick taped up with Steve's help. He's got at least three cracked ribs and a busted lip. He also managed to rip open the stitches she had put in last night. I know he's in pain, but he's pushing through it and looks like a partial mummy for it.

The kids haven't got a clue what's been going on. Crystal has kept them in the pool most of the day and they play like they haven't got a care in the world. I'm glad for it, fewer questions they have, the less I have to lie. I just think some things are a bit too adult for them just yet.

Marissa and I have come to an agreement. I'm sorry for being a super cunt and she's accepted it, saying she's too pregnant and too wrapped up in Brent's OCD to waste time being angry with me anymore. She just advises me to stay away from her husband. Aside from work, that is so not going to be a problem. I have Maverick now and he fills a hole in me that I never thought could be filled. One I tried to drop pills, booze, and sex into for years, that just seemed to be a bottomless hungry pit. Now, I'm feeling full for the first time in my life and it's thanks to him.

I watch him as he watches me. Steve is setting up the fireworks, getting ready to set them off, while the girls play with sparklers in the grass. Brent and Marissa are cuddled up on a blanket, and Kellie and Crystal watch their man. It's almost perfect. I walk over to Maverick and wrap my arms around him gently, mindful of the ribs.

"I love you," I whisper into his chest.

"I love you too," he answers, though it sounds suspicious as he runs a hand through my hair. "What do you want?"

"For once, nothing but this."

Before he can answer me, the first flower explodes in the sky and the kids squeal and dance around. Steve stands proud as the fuses he's set go off in succession, filling the darkness of the desert with all manner of colors.

"Thank you," I mouth to him as he looks over to Maverick and me. He nods with a smile.

❉ ❉ ❉

Little feet in my back wake me in the night. I roll over to find that Angela has crawled into bed with us and she's spread out. I smile, kissing her forehead as I get up. It's like two a.m. and Maverick is down for the count, the poor man has had a long day. I'm thirsty, so I decide to head out to the kitchen to grab a bottle of water. I'm just closing the fridge when I hear someone clear their throat.

Startled, I turn to see Kyle standing there in just his jeans and bare feet, looking like the cat dragged him all over town. Boy, do I not miss those days. Waking up after a bender, your head feeling like it's splitting open, and the world around you is foggy, like the events of the nights gone by.

"Hi," he croaks out, running a hand through his hair uncomfortably. "Where is everybody?"

"Gone. It's after two in the morning, Kyle."

He nods, taking a step toward me and I step back, but the counter and the air in front of me have me pinned with nowhere else to go. "I'm so sorry." He puts up his hands defensively and I see the cuts on them from the fight.

"I'm not the one you need to apologize to, Kyle."

"Yeah? Well, I doubt your new boyfriend is gonna want to hear anything that comes out of my mouth, so I have to put my regrets somewhere."

"Is that what this is? All of this, your outpouring of emotion? You know, you and the guys, you don't own me. I'm not just some toy. I know I put myself out there like a fucking kinky carnival ride, but you all didn't have to buy tickets to the show."

"We've been together three years, Angelica, you and me, on and off, and on and off. Didn't it ever occur to you that maybe I gave a shit about you?"

"No, it occurred to me that you gave a shit about snorting coke off my ass. You never came near me sober, not really. Treated me like a common whore, which I suppose I am, but you know what, I deserve better. Better than you. You, who think that you can waltz into my house, throw down with my guy, and then have the nerve to say it's out of some misguided attempt at showing me you care?" I laugh outright. "Kyle, wake up, the only person you give a shit about is yourself, and maybe Brent on a good day.

He's nodding his head as I speak/ I'm not really angry, just laying it out for him. He needs to understand that what he did, it wasn't cool

"We all have our crosses to bear, you know that as much as any one of us. You know what is was like for me growing up, I've never not been honest with you, and yet, you've never opened up, not really. I mean I have to hear you've got a kid from Steve? Who hides a child for nine years?"

"Someone with reasons to. Take my never opening up as a sign, Kyle, move the fuck on. I have. I'm sober and I want to stay that way. For Maverick, for my daughter, and most importantly, for me. I won't have anyone jeopardize that. It means more to me than just about anything. I'm sorry if you're hurt, but I just can't worry about you. Not anymore, not if you're gonna keep using, keep drinking, womanizing. I just can't waste my time on it."

Kyle studies me as he sits down, his head in his hands. "I know I'm fucked up, alright? I just- Angelica, you were one of the few people who I thought got it. Understood."

"And I do understand. The shit that happened to you, I get it more than most would. But eventually, we all have to put our demons to rest or they are gonna eat us up."

He's quiet for a few moments, then looks up at me. "Are you in love with him?"

"Yeah, I really am." I smile. "More than I ever thought possible, and the kicker is he loves me too. For all my faults, my pomps, and broken parts, he sees me, and he likes what he sees."

"You know if he ever hurts you, I'll kill him. Like seriously, you think that he handed me my ass today, but I was wasted. I won't hesitate to take him out if he ever breaks your heart. None of us would, including Brent." He stands up and looks me square in the face. "You may not think it, but regardless of what you've done, we're family, you, me, Brent, Ringo, and Steve. And we look out for our own." He shakes his head and sighs. "I'm gonna pull my shit together and get out of here. I don't wanna be here when your man wakes up. Somehow, I think two cocks in the hen house is one too many."

"You don't have to-"

He walks over to me and I stiffen as he kisses my forehead. "Yeah. But I do." He walks away, leaving me in the kitchen all alone. I let out a gentle sob, not even sure why, but it seems I need a good cry.

After washing my face, I head back to the bedroom

to find Maverick laying there like a turtle, stuck on its back. I stifle my laugh as he's trying to get up and failing.

"You need a hand?" I whisper, careful not to wake the little one still fast asleep and now taking up much of my side of the bed.

"I need you to quit laughin' at me," he whines, looking up at me with pleading eyes.

The harder I try to stop, the worse it gets. "What do you need?"

"I need up and out of this bed," he demands. There's my Maverick again.

I grab him under the shoulder and by the arm, helping him to stand. "There, now what?"

"Now, you're getting in bed and sleeping with the devil that likes to beat people and I'm gonna go and find a chair." He points to my baby and I smirk.

"She kicked you too?"

"She did something to my ribs," he groans, holding his side.

"I'm sorry, honey." I stand on tiptoe and kiss him lightly.

"I'll be fine," the grouch chews back. I shake my head and open the door.

"Couches and chairs are in the living room," I say, watching him.

"Yeah, I know, that much I can remember."

"Is there anything I can do?" I feel so bad, I know he was defending my honor and all, but now he's broken and there's nothing I can do to make it better.

"Nope, just gonna take time to heal." He looks down at me. "So, is he gone now?"

I nod my head. That damn tablet, please don't let him flip over Kyle kissing me. "Yeah, he was getting his things together and should be gone by now."

"Alright. Sleep well." He's cold again. Back to the domineering prick I've grown to love. Once he rolls things over in his head, maybe he'll talk to me, and maybe I'll just have to go on with my days as per usual. These last few days have been rough for both of us. Now that he's been fired by Imogen Records, I'll need to put him on the payroll, but we need to discuss that, just not right now.

* * *

Morning comes and Maverick is in my chair with his feet up on my coffee table. The poor thing, he doesn't look exactly comfortable. I wonder if I need to move one of the recliners out of the study, maybe that would be better for him.

Doc Peters comes today, and boy, have I got a mouthful for her, but first I need to feed my bleary-eyed little girl and get Maverick up. I'll need him to keep her entertained or at least be awake enough to keep tabs on her while I'm with the doc.

I start breakfast, hoping the smell of fresh sausage sizzling with peppers, potatoes, and onions will wake him. Seems just my moving around the kitchen is enough to poke the bear.

I hear him groan and grit out, "Seriously? It's too early for this..." He tries to roll over and winces. Seems he forgot he was in a chair.

"It's the same time I always make breakfast, shush, you."

"Can you go somewhere else and make breakfast?"

I walk over to him, my hand on my hip. "Listen, mister, I'm cooking, you're eating, I need you to help me out a bit this morning."

He glares up at me, something tells me he thinks I've lost my head. I bend down and tease a kiss from him. "Please, don't be a grouch today."

"You're funny," he mumbles as my lips hover over his.

"I have my moments." I peck his lips again before walking back into the kitchen.

"Right now isn't one of them," he calls after me and I just laugh. Angela comes out of the bedroom a few minutes later, wiping sleep from her eyes.

"Mommy?" she asks with a gravely little tone. "I woke up alone." She's whiny, which makes me wonder if she's feeling okay. I go over to her and feel her head, it's warm.

"It's okay, baby, we're right here. Why don't you go and sit on the couch and keep Maverick company while I finish up breakfast?" Great, just what I need, a broken boyfriend and a sick kid...

32

MAVERICK

ANGELICA HAS THERAPY, ANGELA IS laying on the couch, watching cartoons on a tablet, and me, well, I'm laid up in the fucking chair. I'm broken and will be broke now that I'm fired. I'm in love with a Rockstar who's fucked all the men in her band. Am I pissed? Fuck yeah, I'm pissed. I know in my head and my heart that I can't blame Angelica for the shit she did before me. I'm still in my head though and having a hard time getting out.

I've checked my phone a few times. Angelica has been in with the doc longer than normal. I'm sure she had a lot to get off her chest. A lot has happened since she saw the doc last week. I just hope she's okay. It's killing me to not be able to do anything for her.

Fuck it! I'm hurting, but I got shit to do and can't do it sitting around. Pushing myself to a standing position, I check on Angela, who's fallen asleep, then head to my bedroom. The first thing I do is strip my bed and put my sheets, cover, and pillowcases in the wash. My room is a little less bloody now.

Sitting down at my desk, I begin looking for jobs.

Just because I'm not working doesn't mean I don't have any bills to pay and shit I need. There are a few spots for therapists, a couple rehab centers, I even look at a couple private home jobs. The question is… Can I do another home job after this one? I don't think so. Honestly, I don't think I can go without seeing Angelica for however long I'd be on the job.

I feel Angelica's little arms wrap around my neck before she kisses me. "Hello, Cupcake. Everything okay?"

"Yeah. What are you doing?"

"Looking for a job."

"Why?"

I turn my chair so I can see her face. "Because I have to work. I have an apartment and bills that still have to be paid for."

Angelica walks over and sits on the bed, watching me. "Didn't they pay you enough to not have to worry?"

"No, I had enough to pay my bills and rent. Then I had a little extra to put back for the stuff I need. You know, like flip-flops and clothes when someone broke the washer."

"I don't understand, I've cut ten thousand dollars' worth of checks."

I turn my chair back to the computer and pull up my bank. "Come look, you will see what's coming in and going out. I have nothing to hide."

Angelica walks over to me and is looking at the computer. "You're barely scraping by. So, where the hell did all my money go?"

"I'm not complaining. I'm actually kind of used to living the way I do. As for your money, I don't know."

"I always knew they were a bunch of crooks. Why don't you just stay on here with me?"

I smile, turning back to Angelica and pulling her so she straddles my lap. "I can't, Cupcake. We will kill each other."

"But if you hadn't been fired, it'd been…"

"It would have been the same as it was before Angela. I don't know what I'm doing yet. Right now, the only for sure thing I know is I don't want to take another home job. I never know where I'm going or how long I'll be gone. I couldn't not see you on a regular basis. I have degrees, I just need to figure out a way to use them."

"But you'll be leaving here." I can hear the disappointment in her voice.

"I don't know. I had planned on getting you to where you can handle yourself and Angela without me watching your every move by the three months, but with no money coming in, I don't know what to do."

"What if I said that I don't want you to go?"

"What are you talking about?"

"I don't want you not in my bed. I don't want you not in this house."

I watch her closely and rub at my mouth. "Are you asking me to move in?"

Angelica nods at me. "I think so. It certainly sounds that way. I mean you're already here."

"What would you suggest I do with all the stuff at my condo?"

Angelica looks around, "I think I've got room to spare and Lucille likes it here."

"I brought her to do a job and she did it. I still have to get a job or we'll be at each other's throat."

"Well, what do you want to do?"

"I told you, I want to be able to use my degrees. With you, I use all but two."

"Okay, but that doesn't tell me anything. I don't

know what your degrees are."

"I'm certified as a counselor, physical fitness trainer, nutritionist, and physician's assistant."

"That's a hefty resume you got there, Mister Donovan. That's a lot of letters after your name."

"It's why they hired me for you. Because of that resume."

Angelica looks at me with this lopsided smile. "What if I gave you my den?"

"What am I going to do with a den, Cupcake?"

"See patients."

"Here? I don't think that's a good idea."

"Well, why not? I mean you're gonna go work for somebody else. Have to deal with all their stupid crap and not make nearly what you're worth. Why not be your own boss?"

"I like the my own boss part. The part I don't like is exposing you to people coming and going."

"I need to get used to people again."

I put my hands in the air. "Okay, who would you suggest I see?"

"Start with my bandmates and work your way out from there. I'll even hire you a secretary. Gay, of course."

"Oh, yes, we just need a gay man in this house." I pause and look at her with wide eyes. "I've been trying to figure Ringo out and I'll be damned if you didn't just help me out."

"I have no idea what you're talking about."

"I watch everything and you know I do. I've analyzed each bandmate, except Kyle."

"So about you working from the den?"

"I don't know. It might work, but it might not at the same time. We'd have to completely redo your house and add another door. That way, I could still use the gym and courts like I did with you. I don't know, Angelica, it's a lot to think about. I mean we are talking about cutting into your house and adding shit, blocking off a part to keep people out of the main house."

"I don't know if you realize this, but I have a lot of money. More than I know what to do with."

"You also now have a nine-year-old full time that you still need to figure out school for in the fall."

"No, I already got that worked out."

"School aside, she will need stuff."

"Which won't even put a dent in me. I could pay for her total college tuition right now and not bat an eyelash. *In cash.*"

"I get it. You're fucking loaded and your boyfriend's barely scraping by. If any of your friends knew, they'd laugh their ass off and call me your charity case."

"I guess it's a good thing I don't have any friends and you're far from a charity case."

"What do you call yesterday? They weren't here for me."

"I don't count them. They were being nosy."

"I'm sure Steve, Kellie, and Crystal weren't just being nosy. They are your friends or Steve wouldn't have talked me into staying."

"Yeah, he's good people."

"They are, but so are you. You've come a long way from the stuck-up bitch I met a month go."

"So, are we going to do this thing or what?"

I shake my head. "I don't even know where to start."

"By calling a U-Haul."

"For?"

"Your stuff."

"Cupcake, I don't know if you've noticed, but I'm a bit broken and I'd have to pack shit."

"I've got two hands and like you said, at least three friends. If you haven't noticed, one of them is a really big guy."

"I don't have the energy to argue with you anymore."

"Well, then it's settled, make the calls. I'm sure we can get Ringo to help too. You don't want Brent though, because you'd never get packed."

"Because of his OCD?"

"Oh yeah."

"Figure out when they can help, then I will call and order a couple U-Haul's."

Angelica squeals and bounces in my lap while wrapping her arms around my neck. I cringe in pain. "Cupcake, I love you, but you need to go check on Angela," I grit out.

"Oh, my God. I'm so sorry."

"Just go. I'm sure it's lunch time and I left her asleep on the couch."

Angelica is off, heading for Angela.

❉ ❉ ❉

Angelica is trying to kill me. It's Sunday and we've been packing and moving shit since Thursday. For some reason, she can't understand that I'm broken. Only a couple more rooms, then I'm all moved out.

"Maverick?" I hear Angelica behind me.

I turn to look at her. "Yeah, Cupcake?"

"You have a room devoted entirely to Lucille?" She snickers.

"Uh... Well, yeah." She's found Lucille's room. Lucille spent just about every waking minute in that room. There are four cat trees, one for each corner of the room. I built walkways and stairs along the walls. She's got plants, toys, plenty of beds all over the place. Her favorite is the swing I made her.

"Boy, Maverick, you really do love your pussy... Cat," Steve says.

"I treat them with the respect they deserve." I chuckle.

Angelica smirks. "Maybe we should get Lucille a couple little playmates. I mean you got all the stuff."

"Let's not and say we did." I turn away and start placing more shit in boxes. Steve, Kellie, and Ringo have been helping. They are doing about all the lifting. Angelica is doing most of the cleaning and I'm working on packing everything into boxes.

After packing up the last couple of rooms, Steve, Kellie, and Ringo take off toward the house. Angelica and I are cleaning up the rest of the condo. She's in the other room, we haven't really had as much time to talk as normal, but that is probably a good thing. I've been in this place since I moved to Vegas. It was a quiet space, far from the crazy Vegas lifestyle. Now I wonder what I've agreed to, upheaving my sanctuary and moving in with a Rockstar.

33

ANGELICA

WHEN I SET MY MIND TO SOMETHING, I run with it. Moving Maverick in took all of four days. Well, getting his stuff here, that is. Most of it is in the four-car garage that I never use. I've got Ringo, Steve, and Brent here, emptying out the back four bedrooms to be used as office space and exam rooms for him, as well as the in-law apartment that I never did have a need for. We haven't figured out just what we're doin' with it all, but we figure once the space is empty we can see it better. I'm thankful to the guys for stepping up to help. They seem to really want to, and they seem to like Maverick, for the most part. Brent is still as aloof as ever, but that's his way, and we haven't heard from Kyle. He's staying away, which both saddens and fills me with relief at the same time, as something tells me that if those two are in the same room, it will get bloody again.

With the guys here, Angela has had full-time playmates in Steve's daughters and Crystal has even begun some summer reading with them to get them ready for the fall. I talked to her on the fourth and she says that she'll be happy to take Angela on as her student. She's got a Masters in teaching and has been homeschooling the girls since they were old enough. It was her initial job, before she got *involved* with Kellie and Steve romantically. Angela likes her, which is a plus for us all.

Kellie and Marissa have been here most of the time too, which is sorta weird. Not Kellie, but Marissa, seeing as we don't have the best track record, but with me sober and her slowed down by this pregnancy, we have begun to find things we have in common.

Her drive and ambition is admirable, even though she's been unable to work since getting pregnant, she's continued to sing. Her demo is actually *really* good. I understand now why Christy was so willing to take her on if I can't get my shit together. She could handle my range and complement Brent without batting an eyelash, while at the same time, bringing a fresh voice to the band. Maybe I'll let her cut a song or two on the next album. I'll have to talk to Brent and the guys, but I think they'll be on board.

Even with everyone around, I've been keeping up with my chores for the most part, though I've had help in the cooking department. Kellie knows her way around a kitchen and likes to toss me out and do the cooking. When she does, though, I've had to remind her that I have dietary restrictions and she laughs, goading me about Maverick and his rules. I just smile and go on my way.

It's Tuesday and I've just finished tending to the plants in the greenhouse. I've got tomatoes, bell peppers, chili peppers, lettuces, carrots, potatoes, and all kinds of herbs growing like wildfire in there this season. Who'd have thought that I'd have a green thumb, but it seems

I'm good with plants. Like Lucille, they're something to talk to that doesn't talk back. I head into my room to change into my gym clothes and find a box on my bed with a note. The note is from Maverick.

Here ya go, Cupcake. Just a little somethin' for the week ahead.
Love,
Maverick

I scrunch up my nose as I look inside and find a stack of dark chocolate Hershey bars, a bag of Hershey kisses, and a box of Midol, just enough doses to add to my pill case for the week. Maverick has been laying out my pills this way for about two weeks now. On Monday, he sets them out and I fill my case and he trusts me to take them as I am supposed to. So far, I've been good. I feel better when I take them, so I always remember to. I look at the calendar on my wall, it's the eighteenth already? Where has the month gone? He's packed this box in preparation for my period. It's sweet, but it hasn't started yet. What with all the running around and the stress of Angela being here, I'm sure it's just my hormones being whacked out. I couldn't be pregnant, we've been super careful.

❈ ❈ ❈

"Did you get it?" I ask Kellie as she comes into my room and nods her head yes. Reaching into her bra, she pulls out a plastic baggie with a brand-new pregnancy test inside. It's Friday, and I've still seen no signs of my period, so I had her smuggle the thing in to me, as I can't very well tell Maverick. He would lose his shit.

"Are you sure you aren't just late?" she asks me, handing it over nervously.

"Kell, I haven't missed a period since I was fourteen, and I was pregnant that time." I look at the test. "Christ, how did I end up here?"

"You two do fuck like rabbits." She snickers, looking around. "I'm gonna go raid your closet, you've gotta have shoes I can steal, at least then I have a reason to be in here."

I nod, heading for the bathroom and shutting the door. My chest is heaving and I feel like I'm about to die. Fucking anxiety, and of course, I can't even manage to pee, I'm so tense.

"C'mon…" I scold myself, holding the little stick between my legs. Finally, I do what needs doing and now, I have to wait five minutes. I can't just sit here, making myself crazier than I already am. I head out of the bathroom and to my walk-in closet to find Kellie rummaging through all my shoes.

"I love that you don't own a heel under four inches. Steve thinks my obsession with Jimi Choo is unhealthy." She grins, parading around in my stilettos.

"Feel free to borrow whatever you want, just take care of them."

"But, of course." She swoons, picking up several pairs. "What are you gonna do if it's positive?" she asks, more serious now.

I run my hands through my hair, then down my face, blowing out air. "I- I just don't know. I mean he doesn't want kids. He wanted me to go on birth control, and I assured him that we'd be fine with condoms, and we've been burning through them like every time, I mean…" I stop. Thinking back to the fourth of July when we were in the shower. "Oh, God. I know when this could have happened. We slipped up and I don't think even he realizes it," I moan.

Kellie puts down the shoes and hugs me. "It's okay, Angelica, if you are and he doesn't step up, we're here for you, no matter what you decide to do."

"There's no deciding. I have a *nine-year-old,* remember? If I were willing to abort, I *wouldn't.*"

Kellie hugs me tighter. "We'll get through this, I promise you."

I pull from her and wipe the tears from my face, heading back into the bathroom and picking up the test. I look down at it and it reads,

PREGNANT.

And the world goes dark.

* * *

When next I open my eyes, Maverick is sitting across from me and Kellie is looking me over. "What happened?" I ask, sitting up, my head thumping.

"You fainted and cracked your head on the sink," Kellie answers as Maverick gets up.

"Just give her a moment," Kellie barks before looking back to me.

"Does he?" I mouth while she's blocking his line of sight.

"I already got rid of it," Kellie whispers as she shines a light in my eyes. "Follow my finger."

"I'm not a cat," I muse, but do as she asks.

"Okay, I'd say there's no concussion. She's all yours, professor." Kellie smiles, letting Maverick have access to me. I sit up a little straighter, not sure what I'm going to do.

"What happened?" he asks, towering over me a moment before sitting down.

"Apparently, I fainted."

"Okay, but why?"

I swallow. "Would you get me a glass of water? My mouth is really dry."

He looks at Kellie, who nods and leaves the room. There goes my shield. I just stare at my hands folded against my stomach. I still can't believe I've got a life growing inside me. How the hell am I supposed to tell this man?

I clear my throat as he stares at me and just as I'm about to open my mouth to speak, Kellie comes running back in with a bottle of water.

"Here ya go. I'll be just outside if ya need me," she stammers, looking at us both before hightailing it out of the room. Maverick's eyes follow her out, then sail back to me, then the door once more.

"What's going on?" he asks in an overly curious tone.

I sip the water and hold the bottle in my lap. "Um, I need to tell you something. Something you're really... Not gonna like."

He nods his head. "Okay."

"Um, I... See, you and me... Fuck," I hiss, gulping down more water.

He wipes his mouth, I know I'm frustrating him. "Would you spit it out already?"

"I'm knocked up."

"You're what?"

"I think you heard me," I whisper, looking at him.

He nods his head, standing up and wiping his hands on his thighs. He makes to say something, then just shakes his head and walks out.

34

MAVERICK

PREGNANT? She can't be fucking pregnant. I wouldn't have messed up that bad. I've always used protection or pulled out. FUCK! I told her to get on birth control. Who am I kidding? I should have gotten snipped when I first decided I didn't want kids. I can't believe I got her pregnant. She's barely sober, how can she handle being pregnant?

I stormed out, leaving Angelica in our room. The only thing I knew when she told me was I couldn't breathe and I needed to get out of there. I damn near plowed over Kellie to get away.

Finally feeling like I'm far enough from the house, I take a seat on the ground. It's hotter than the Devil's balls out here, but it's the only place to get the time I need. Of course, it's hot. We're in the deserts of Nevada in the middle of July.

I'm not even alone fifteen minutes and Steve's found me. First, I see the shadow and then water pours all over me before he sits down.

"The fuck, dude?"

"I was afraid you were gonna melt," Steve says, tossing another bottle of water in my lap.

"I assure you, I'd have been fine. What do you want?"

"I've been where you're at. Did you know my oldest is sixteen?"

"Pregnant and not wanting kids? I did, but I do my research and pay attention to the people around me."

"I didn't even have time to think about whether I wanted them or not. I was a baby *having* babies."

"I have reasons that I don't want kids."

"And I'm guessing it's the same reasons you don't drink or smoke. People in your line of work have their reasons."

"Most do, but usually the ones in my line of work have done the shit themselves. I never have, just witnessed it."

"Sometimes, that's all it takes."

"Maybe so, but it was enough to tell me I couldn't do the parent thing. Hell, even if I could, I don't have a job. No fucking money coming in. About a thousand left to my name. Still not a clue what I'm doing exactly."

Steve chuckles. "You got a woman bending over backward to give you everything you need. She'll get you started. What you do with it is up to you."

"You don't get it. I've never depended on anyone in my life."

"How about I loan you the money?"

"Hell no."

"No, hear me out. I'd be a silent partner. You give me a number, however much you need, and I'll have the lawyers draw it up, then give you a length of time to pay it back."

"That's just it, I'm not sure what I'm doing yet. I

know what Angelica wants me to do, but I've never stayed still like I am right now for more than six months at a time."

"You'll adjust. If you want to."

"She wants me to work a desk job. I've never worked a desk job in my life."

"She didn't say anything about a desk job. She's willing to literally knock out walls so you can do whatever you need to do."

"Only because I'm not willing to have people coming and going around her and Angela. I can't take the chance of someone still being messed up and bringing it around her. I would never forgive myself. Then what happens if you all have to travel? I just cancel my appointments, pick up, and go?"

Steve turns to me, voice taking on a more serious tone. "I don't see much travel for her future."

"What are you talking about?"

"Kellie never came with me on the road when she was pregnant. There were just too many risk factors."

"She isn't always going to be pregnant. Then what? I become the stay at home daddy? I don't know if you noticed, but I'm not good with kids."

"You think I was at fifteen? Hell, I was angry, resentful. Kell and I had a shotgun wedding."

"If I'm not ready for a kid, I'm sure as hell not ready for marriage."

"I'm not saying she is either, but it's something you're going to have to talk about. Because something tells me that she's going to have that baby. With or without you."

I run a hand through my hair. "Yeah, I'm sure of that too. I'm gonna stay out here for a bit. Will you, um, make sure she eats? It's that time for her."

Steve shrugs his shoulders, getting up. "You do what you gotta do, man. But if you want my opinion, for what it's worth, just pull the trigger because in the long run, it's worth it."

After Steve walks away, I spend a few more hours in that same spot, thinking about everything. A lot has happened in less than two months. I've fallen for my client, knocked her up, I'm jobless, and apparently, I'm a dominant prick, but none of that seems to matter.

Finally, I think, just maybe, I can face Angelica and begin heading back to the house. On the hike to the back, I pull out my phone and bring up Spotify because it can usually help clear my head. A song starts just as I'm about to the house and it screams everything I'm feeling, but just haven't been able to explain.

I'm brought out of my thoughts by a voice saying, "*You*, sit." It's Marissa, she's sitting on the stairs.

"What the hell are you doing out here?"

"Do as you're *told*," she says as she pats the stair next to her.

I watch her, then look toward the doors before looking back to her. I'm not looking to fight anymore right now. "Thanks, but I think I'll stand." Marissa attempts to get up but can't on her own. So, being the man I am, I go over to help her up. "Jesus, are you trying to hurt yourself?"

She grabs my wrists and places my hands on her belly. I try to jerk back, but the girl ain't letting go and I don't want to hurt her. "This is the most terrifying thing imaginable. I was fourteen weeks pregnant when I found out. No symptoms, no signs, and no opportunity to make a choice. I never wanted kids. So, I understand, probably more than anyone. I was terrified of pushing my family's crazy onto a new generation, but you know

216

what I realized? If I could go through hell and be okay, then I know these babies are going to be fine. Because we are going to love them the way we weren't."

I bite down on my lip as one of the babies kicks my hand through Marissa's belly. I just kind of watch her belly as a tear begins to fall. "It's not even been two months."

Marissa laughs and everything jiggles. "Brent and I were married after four hours and pregnant right out of the gate. Time is relative. When you know, you just know. He knew, and she does too…"

"Thank you, but I need to cut this short. I have somewhere to be and I'm sure your husband is pacing the floors waiting for you."

Marissa smiles and nods her head. "You do what you need to do."

With a curt nod, I'm up the stairs and heading into the house. I damn near run into Steve as he's dancing around the living room. "Can't talk. Gotta go," I shout and keep busting ass to the place I left Angelica, in our bed. I stop just outside the door and take a deep breath before walking in.

Shutting the door behind me, I take a look around. Angelica is in the bed, curled up on her side and there's a tray of food that hasn't been touched. I go over to my side and move the tray before slipping off my shoes and climbing into the bed beside her. I pull Angelica into my arms. "I'm sorry for being a jackass, Cupcake."

Angelica wraps her arms around me and holds on for dear life. "I'm sorry."

"What are you sorry for? This is my fault, not yours."

"I know this is the last thing you wanted."

I shake my head and pull my phone out of my

pocket. "I have something I need you to listen to since I can't carry a tune in a bucket." I hit play and *In Case You Didn't Know* by Brett Young begins to come on. I shut my phone off once the song is over.

Angelica sits up, staring down at me and she's crying. "I don't wanna do this without you, but I'm prepared to. Sure, you love me, but it's not fair for me to force you into this."

She's going to make me spell it all out for her. Here goes nothing. "Cupcake, I've been crazy for you from day two. You pulled yourself out of the pool, naked as all get out, and marched up to me like you were the boss. Little did you know, *I* was the boss and you'd like it. You sparked something inside me that nobody has ever even come close to. So, what I'm saying now is… I'm going to suck at this relationship thing, even more at the daddy thing, but by God, I'm going to be beside you. I'm not going anywhere because just like you, I can't live this life without you." I watch her closely and she's just blubbering.

Angelica wipes at her face. "Do you mean that?"

"Do you really think I'd have said it if I didn't mean it?"

Angelica rolls her shoulders almost defiantly. "You say a lot of things, but if you mean that, then marry me. I mean will you marry me?"

"Aren't I supposed to ask that?"

"Has anything we've done so far been normal? Besides, we are in the twenty-first century."

"No, and not for my lack of trying. You are fucking complicated, but I'm stuck. You ready to go tonight?"

"I have nothing to wear." She stares at me wide eyed.

"We are in *Vegas*."

~THE END~

Don't be sad, there's more to come, Steve's life is about to take a turn, and he's gonna be needing his friends more now than ever before...

Steven Falcone aka Steve Vicious is the infamous *Fallen Angels* drummer. He seems to have it all - money, a gorgeous wife, three beautiful daughters, and a sexy live-in girlfriend. He's managed to take the open relationship mainstream in a world where it's still very taboo.

The problem?

Steve wants something like monogamy again, but Kellie is into the D/s scene and Steve worries that their vanilla life may not be enough... Can he learn to embrace his darker side to give the love of his life the spice she needs or will he lose her forever to a world he just doesn't understand?

Read on for a Chapter Preview of

TATTED UP AND TIED DOWN.

A Sex, Drugs and Rock Romance Book 3

Coming in September 2017.

1

STEVE

"I MISS YOU, DADDY," Peggy Sue, my oldest, says into the phone and my heart breaks. She's been in Colorado for the last six months to keep her away from the prying eyes of the press. See, she's having herself a baby, which should make for a joyous event, but she's just this side of sixteen. How pissed was I when I found out? Ever seen a bear get shot and not die? Yeah, I was about right there. The father? A good for nothing rocker from one of the opening bands while we were touring in Australia. We found out just after we got home, adding to an already smoldering fire.

See, it hasn't been all wine and roses for Kellie, Crystal, and me. Not for a while. Three's company, but four, five, and six? Well, that's not sitting with me like it used to. Here lies our dilemma. Kellie likes our arrangement. I, however, want something different, something more like monogamy, but how do I get that and not break up our family?

"Daddy?" Peggy Sue asks, pulling me back from my thoughts.

"Yeah, honey?" I answer with a catch in my throat.

"I said I miss you." She sounds so tiny on the other end.

"I know, honey. Maybe Crys and I will come up this weekend. Bring the girls."

"Not mom?" she asks curiously.

"She sees Damien," I deadpan and she goes quiet. Peggy Sue is at the age where we've pretty much made her aware of our lifestyle. Not the nitty gritty, but the overall gist of it.

"Oh," her answer tells me she's got the same opinion I'm beginning to have, that it's time Damian take a long walk off a short pier.

"But it'll be good, yeah?"

"Yeah." She sighs. "You should see me, I'm as big as a house."

"Any word from Harrison Lagrange?" That's the name of the sperm donor. He hadn't said one word to her when we tracked him down and slapped him with the papers for responsibility. Seems he's just eighteen, so no legal charges could be filed, but his response has been to send money every month and that is it.

"Nope, just the checks, but they have gotten bigger."

"What's bigger?"

"This last one was for ten thousand."

I suck air in through my teeth. "Have you deposited it?"

"No, Daddy, I've not deposited any of them, been putting them aside like you said, for the lawyer, for after the baby comes, just like you said."

"Good girl," I say, swishing my Scotch, staring at the fire I've made. "Good girl. I'll talk to your mom, maybe she'll forgo her weekend to see you. If not, at least it'll be us. Okay?"

"Alright, Daddy. Oomph…"

"What?" I ask with concern.

"He's a kicker is all. Must be feeding time." Peggy Sue laughs. "I'm gonna go. I love you, Daddy."

"Love you too, my Peggy Sue."

She giggles, hanging up, and I throw my tumbler at the fireplace, smashing it with a growl.

"What *are* you doing?" I hear Kellie and turn, seeing her looking freshly fucked in the doorway. She was with *him* tonight, and God knows who else. Leaving Crystal and me with the girls.

"You're home early," I bark, not quite drunk enough to want to deal with her.

"And you're drinking? With the girls home?" she spits. "I thought we talked out this?"

"Damn it, woman, what I do in my own home is my fucking business, I'm not drunk, I had two drinks. Needed them after the day I had, is that okay with you?"

She walks over to me, her steps tell me she's probably got some good bruises on her ass from tonight, and I shake my head as she looks me in the eyes. She submits for her Dom, but here at home, she's always aggressive. "What happened?"

"Just a rough one. Between Brent and Marissa getting ready to have the babies and Angelica and Maverick just coming back from Aspen after getting hitched last month, it's just getting to be too much. Everyone has so much going on, it's like they've all forgotten we have an album to promote, and no one is even talking new material. Even Ringo is in his own little world, which is not like him.

"Bear, it's life. We all have one, maybe it's time you got back to yours." She puts her arms around me and

3

fishes for a kiss. I groan against her lips, tasting the blackberry lip balm. She smells sweet and clean. Damian's rule, she always comes home to me properly bathed, no matter how badly he's used her.

I grab her by the ass and she winces then purrs. She likes the pain as I push my cock against her stomach. I'm not hard, but it's still a beast. She knows just what I need though, as she unzips my jeans and pulls me toward the couch.

She sits and slides my cock into her pert little mouth, wrapping her lips tightly around it, her hands stroking the length that doesn't fit down her throat. I grab her hair and pound into her mouth. Fuck, it feels good. I wrap my hand into her dirty blonde hair and pop her off my dick. She looks at me, confused until I rip open her blouse, sending the buttons flying.

"Hmm, someone's in a mood," she whispers.

"Shut up," I grit out, hiking up her skirt and pushing her panties aside as I pull up her leg to open her pussy to me. I drive my thick, pulsing cock into her and she whimpers from the force as I lift her off the floor, wrapping her legs around my hips. We haven't fucked like this in a while. I've been too busy with the band and we've been fighting a lot, but tonight, I'm just too fucking horny to care about any of that. It doesn't last long, but when I feel her clench up around me, I know I've done my part and can come too. I drop her down on the couch and zip up my pants, leaving her panting and astonished as I go clean up.

ABOUT THE AUTHORS

J. Haney was born and raised in Kentucky, currently residing in Greenup County, Kentucky with her family, where she is the proud momma to Jessalyn Kristine and co-owner of Proud Momma Designs, which she runs with her amazing Momma. J. Haney's work tends to lean toward sweet and sexy, with suspenseful undertones, giving her readers something to hold onto.

S.I. Hayes was born and bred in New England, currently living in Ohio. Running around Connecticut, she used all of her family and friends as inspiration for her many novels. When not writing Paranormal Drama or Erotic Romance she can be found drawing one of many fabulous book covers or teasers. To see them check out her website. www.sihayes.com

The pair met while working for a former publisher and became fast friends, their split dynamics and views on life, family, and love in general led to the idea of *A County Fair Romance*. They now bring you *A Sex, Drugs and Rock Romance*. They do hope to bring you more of their shenanigans in the months to come, so keep your eyes open and a fresh pair of panties close by, you know, just in case.

J. Haney Links:
Website Facebook Street Team Twitter Pinterest
Goodreads Instagram TSU Google +
YouTube Spotify

S.I. Hayes Links:
A Writer's Mind, More or Less
The 131 Preview Review
Facebook Website Twitter

75797970R00130

Made in the USA
Columbia, SC
29 August 2017